Harriet
and
Emilie

Eleanor Watkins

Grace & Down
PUBLISHING

First published 2022 by Grace and Down Publishing
an imprint of Malcolm Down Publishing Limited

British Library Cataloguing-in-Publication Data
A catalogue record for this book is available from the British Library.

ISBN 978-1-915046-24-6

Cover design by Esther Kotecha
Art direction by Sarah Grace

Printed in the UK

Part One
Harriet and Emilie

Harriet

I can't even remember a time when Emilie was not there. I don't believe she was born at Compton Manor, but it could not have been long after her birth that she and her mother Janina came. Janina became our cook, ruling the Compton kitchen with a rod of iron and a large basting spoon, which, I learned, struck fear into the heart of any lesser mortal who might invoke her displeasure. There were times, Emilie told me, when that same basting spoon was applied to the rear of Emilie's combination suit. I winced in sympathy as she told me; the corrective measures I received came in the form of one of Nanny's slippers, and both Nanny and her slippers were on the soft side.

My first real memory of Emilie was from the day I escaped the day nursery, found my way to the back stairs and down into the lower regions of the manor house. I must have been between three and four years old, born, as Nanny sometimes remarked, in the very first year of the new twentieth century. I have no memory of the day of the week or the time of year; all were much the same in the ordered world of the nursery.

I had woken early from my afternoon nap; I saw that Nanny was still dozing in her comfortable rocking chair, with her knitting in her lap. Annie the nursemaid had time off during nap hour and was nowhere to be seen. I swiftly climbed down from my bed and made my escape. My bare feet pattered along corridors and around corners, until I came to a twisty, dim staircase that invited me to descend. Steadying myself with one hand

4

against the wall, I carefully lowered my short legs from step to step, down and down. There was a lonely moment when I was out of sight of the landing above and could see nothing but more steps ahead of me. These were bare wood, nothing like the big front staircase, with its covering of green carpet held in place by golden stair rods: the stairs I travelled carried in someone's arms or led by someone's hand. These steps were cold and hard and seemed to go on for ever. I hesitated for a moment, thinking of the warm nursery and my familiar toys. Then I went on.

I had reached the bottom of the stairs and stood in a stone-paved passage. Huge green baize doors were a little way ahead, barring my way. The floor was so cold that my bare toes curled. I stood against the wall and rubbed one foot on the other to try to get a little warmth. A faint hum of voices sounded from behind the doors. There was a clash of pans and a faint smell of cooking food – gravy, cabbage, and other things I couldn't recognise. I was hungry. When Nanny woke, it would be time for nursery tea. But, first, I would see what lay behind the green doors.

Before I could reach them, they opened a little way and someone slipped through, releasing a burst of sound and steamy warmth before they closed again. It was a very small person, my size, a little girl, who stopped short when she saw me standing there in the passageway. We stood and stared at each other. She had fine flaxen hair escaping from a floppy bow, a slightly grubby and wrinkled pinafore, striped stockings and button boots. She stared at me for a long time, especially at my bare feet. Even in the dim light, I could see that her eyes were very blue, as blue as the bluebells in our copse.

My tummy rumbled. I wondered if the other girl could tell me where to find something to eat. But before we could say a word to each other, the green doors flew open again and a tall man came through. I didn't know him, although I thought I'd seen him before. He had carroty hair, freckles and a nose that turned up at the end. He didn't see me at first.

He said, 'Emilie, you're going to catch it if your ma notices you've run off again! Come back before she sees— Whoa! Who's this?'

5

He had seen me and his mouth fell open in surprise. Then he grinned, his cheeks squeezed together so that all the freckles ran into one. 'I do believe it's little Lady Harriet!' he said. 'And with no shoes and stockings! I bet Nanny doesn't know you're down here!'

I shook my head. I liked him, and I remembered I must mind my manners. 'Please could I have something to eat?'

He laughed, throwing back his head. The little girl, Emilie, laughed as well, just because he was laughing. I might have laughed too, but my feet were getting colder and colder.

Then he stopped, bent down to me and said, 'Look, chicken, you're not supposed to be down here. I'm going to get one of the girls to take you back to the nursery, or someone's going to be in hot water.'

He took me by the hand, and shooing Emilie in front of us, went through the doors. Suddenly, we were in a big, steamy, noisy room, with people bustling about, stirring, chopping, carrying pans and talking in loud voices. When they saw me, a silence fell and a lot of startled faces stared down at me.

'Well, I'm jiggered!' said a big girl, with a white cap on her brown curls. 'What's she doing down here then, Henry?'

'Found her outside the door, in the passage,' said the freckle-faced young man. 'Says she's hungry, and could she have something to eat?'

For some reason, everyone thought this was very funny. All of them laughed. Then they stopped laughing and looked at one another. A plump lady put down a big yellow bowl, came over and picked me up, sitting down with me in her lap. 'You are not supposed to be down here, you know, little lady. Polly will take you back. *Ach*, child, your feet are freezing!'

I liked the plump lady in the big white apron. Maybe she would give me something to eat.   'I'm hungry,' I said, whining.

'*Ach*, I'd give you and my Emilie a spice cookie. But it is time now for your tea, upstairs.'

I noticed that Emilie was standing close by. I instantly understood that this was Emilie's mother. I didn't want to go upstairs. The freckle-faced man called Henry had disappeared, and the big, curly haired girl called Polly, a kitchen maid, took me from Emilie's mama. I squirmed in protest, but she was strong and held me fast all the way upstairs and into the nursery. Nanny was still asleep, but she awoke with a start when Polly deposited me on the rug and left the room, closing the door behind her.

'Oh, you're awake already, pet. Let's get your shoes and stockings on, and brush your hair, then I'll ring for tea. Did you have a lovely sleep?'

I never said a word to anyone about going down to the kitchens, and nobody there said anything either. I thought longingly of the spice cookie Emilie would be enjoying while I ate my own tea. I did not know what a spice cookie was, but I thought it sounded much nicer than my bread and butter with gooseberry jam, and plain sponge cake.

CHAPTER

Harriet

Once I knew there was another little girl in the house, I felt drawn to her like a magnet. Everyone else there was grown up: Mama and Papa, my big sisters and my brother, Nanny, the ladies' maids, housemaids and the other servants hidden away in that busy, noisy, mysterious other world behind the green baize doors downstairs. Sometimes I was taken to tea with other little girls like me. We would wear our best smocked and frilled dresses, and play with wax-cheeked dolls similarly attired, while our nannies sat together drinking tea and exchanging gossip. But I longed for a real everyday playmate, and could not understand why Emilie and I were mostly kept apart.

'*Why* can't I go down to play with Emilie?' I would demand for the dozenth time.

'Because you are a little lady and she is not,' Nanny would reply.

I stamped my foot. 'I'm *not* a little lady! Ladies are big! I'm a little girl and Emilie is a little girl. I want to play with her!'

'Then want must be your master,' said Nanny, which was her standard answer whenever I wanted something forbidden.

Nanny was infuriating. I loved her and sometimes hated her with equal measure. She was old now, her hair white and a little wispy, although she had once had luxuriant tresses that fell below her waist. This I knew from a photograph she had shown me of herself as a young girl.

Nanny had taken care of my father and his brothers and sisters, and then my own older siblings. She had been taken out of her retirement in a snug little estate cottage to look after me, born several years after my brother. I'd once heard my mother remark to a friend that she hoped Nanny would 'last out' until I was grown. Nanny was old, and sometimes forgetful, but she still had a will of iron.

I appealed to my mother one evening when, bathed and dressed in my sailor-suit frock and with a big navy-blue bow in my hair, I'd been deposited in the drawing room downstairs for the customary daily hour with my parents.

'Mama, I would like to play with Emilie.'

Mama smiled her kind, rather vague smile, which caused tiny wrinkles to appear at the corners of her eyes. Her hair had a few little streaks of white in it, which her maid Dora covered with some dark stuff from a bottle. Mama's hair would look beautiful and lustrously brunette for a while, until some more white streaks appeared. She wore beautiful dresses – tea gowns, she called them – that were soft rose pinks and apple greens.

'Sweetheart, it will be bedtime when you go back upstairs.'

'I don't mean now. I mean tomorrow. Or some other day.'

She sighed gently and reached out to pull me close to her on the sofa. 'I'll see if I can arrange for you to go to visit Olivia at Burke Hall. Or maybe the little Beaumont girls.'

I pulled away. 'I don't want to. I want to play with Emilie. Why can't I?'

Mama sighed again and appealed to my father, hidden away in his armchair, behind the day's newspaper. 'Rupert, can you talk to her?'

My father rustled the paper rather irritably and then lowered it. 'What is the trouble now?'

His hair was quite grey, slicked back, but, strangely, his thick moustache had remained brown.

'And who is Emilie?'

'Cook's girl. Harriet seems obsessed with her.' She paused. 'Rupert, would it hurt if they played together now and then?'

Papa wore eyeglasses for reading now. He lowered his head and looked at Mama over the tops of them. He seemed to be weighing up the question seriously. I held my breath.

He said, 'I hardly think an occasional encounter would cause any harm. Cook seems a decent kind of woman and has given excellent service. I am sure she has taught her child well.'

Having delivered his verdict, he gave the paper another shake, and retired behind it.

I let out my breath and said, 'Thank you, Papa!' I didn't dare rush over and fling my arms round his neck, as I would have liked. Instead, I said again, 'Thank you, Papa.'   He rustled the paper dismissively. His opinion was given; the subject was closed. There were far more important matters on his mind.

I was ecstatic. I would have spent every waking moment with Emilie had I been allowed. But our visits were rationed: an hour here, an hour there, always supervised by the nursemaid, Annie. We made the most of the time, building houses, stables and menageries on the nursery floor with my wooden blocks and animals. We'd take it in turns, shrieking, to gallop on the rocking-horse and we'd paste pictures into scrapbooks. But most of all, I loved the rare times when we could play downstairs in the big, steamy kitchen, cutting out our own 'biscuits' with scraps of pastry, helping to pop peas out of their pods or eating one of Janina's spice cookies.

A faint air of disapproval overshadowed our times in the nursery. Nanny never fully accepted the situation and considered Emilie's presence an affront to the traditional way of doing things. But downstairs, it seemed all good humour and laughter, unfailing kindness to me, and plenty of banter and jokes between the servants. I didn't understand the jokes but I didn't care a jot.

Emilie and I discovered that we were the same age, almost to the day. Our birthdays fell in the same week of the same month of the same year – a year that was the beginning of a brand new century. Other than that, we couldn't have been more different. She was fair and rather serious; I was dark, impatient and quick with my tongue.

I went to Emilie's fifth birthday party: a noisy occasion round the kitchen table. Her birthday cake, made by her mother, was called a *Prinzregententorte* and, on it, five candles burned brightly. The staff sang

'Happy Birthday' and presented Emilie with little gifts – a hair ribbon, a spinning-top, a set of little wooden dolls carved by Henry, and a pair of warm, knitted mittens. Emilie was a great pet with them all.

My own party was in the downstairs drawing room, with me and my guests in stiffly starched party dresses and ringletted hair. We ate dainty sandwiches, jellies, and strawberries and cream in pink-glass dishes. Strawberries were out of season but some greenhouse-grown ones had been specially ordered. We played party games, musical chairs, pass the parcel and postman's knock. Olivia James-Clark and her brothers came, so did the little Beaumont girls and the four children from Landsdown Hall.

Emilie was not invited.

Harriet

Time passed. By the time I reached my seventh birthday, I was made of sterner stuff. When I heard that celebrations were being planned along the lines of my fifth birthday party, I stoutly protested. 'I don't like those kinds of parties. I don't want one.'

My mother sighed. I was growing into a child with a well-developed stubborn streak, and she was sometimes at a loss to know how to deal with me. But she acknowledged it would be of no use inviting little guests if their young hostess were to spend the whole time glowering in a corner.

'Well then, what would you like to do?'

I said the first thing that came into my head. 'A picnic.'

'A picnic? In March?'

Now that I'd had the idea, it was beginning to grow on me. 'Yes. With pie and fruit cake and flasks of soup. Like a shooting picnic.'

'But it's not even shooting season!' My mother looked at me helplessly. 'And the little girls may not care for that kind of thing.'

'I don't want any little girls', I said. 'Just me and Emilie.'

And that's what we got. Accompanied by Nanny, wrapped in shawls and grumbling mightily, Emilie and I were driven in the dogcart. Emilie was squeezed in beside the groom in front, Nanny and I were equally crushed together in the other seat, back to back with the other two. We arrived at our chosen destination, the bluebell copse, although it was too early for bluebells to be in flower, and there we picnicked.

Hobbs the groom set up a folding table and chairs, and we solemnly ate our provisions. A chilly wind whistled around our ears and rattled the bare hazel branches, and Nanny declared that it would be the death of her. In truth, I looked forward to getting home to the nursery fire myself, not that I would admit as much to anyone.

When the food was finished, I announced my intention of further activity. Powdery, yellow catkins swung from the hazels and, at the far end of the copse, there was a patch of marshy ground where I knew there would be pussy willow, its paler yellow balls of fluff as soft and downy as day-old chicks.

'We'll get some for the nursery,' I said.

'Whatever next?' grumbled Nanny. 'They drop their pollen everywhere and make me sneeze. Be quick about it, then. Don't expect me to come traipsing after you. And stay in sight.' She retreated to the dogcart to wrap herself in an extra rug and complain about her chilblains.

Emilie and I made our way through the copse, our booted feet soundless on the soft leaf mould. Near the damp bit, it was squidgy and we sank in a little. It didn't take long to gather an armful of pale yellow willow catkins. I glanced back at the dogcart, visible through the bare trees.

'Let's not go back yet,' I said. 'Let's go across to the big wood and explore!'

We seldom had time together out of doors; the sense of freedom had gone to my head.

Emilie's cheeks were pink from the cold and tendrils of hair, yellow as the catkins, escaped from under her woollen hood. She began to say doubtfully, 'But Nanny said—'

'Pooh to Nanny!' I said grandly. 'Hobbs is smoking. Look, you can see the smoke going up, and I bet Nanny is too.'

'Nanny doesn't smoke!'

'She used to. She told me. A pipe. Women smoked pipes where she came from. I bet she's smoking one now.'

We burst into a fit of giggles at the thought of Nanny puffing on a pipe. I laid down the bunch of pussy willow, grabbed Emilie's mittened hand and pulled her away from the copse, across a field to the fringes of the big wood beyond. I half expected an irate shout, yet there was nothing but the wind in the trees and the cawing of a couple of crows, flapping their way to the wood.

We pulled up panting at the edge of the trees. Tall oaks, beeches and ash trees, with just the first hints of budding leaves on their bare branches, stretched away into the dim mysterious depths. Inviting green pathways between the trees were bordered by last year's limp, brown bracken and bare bramble bushes. I longed to follow one of those pathways to see where it led.

But there was a barrier, a wire fence around the perimeter with fearsome looking barbs along the top.

'We can't get in,' I said, my voice flat with disappointment.

'I don't think we're meant to,' said Emilie nervously. 'There's a gamekeeper who carries a gun to shoot poachers and trespassers. He comes into the kitchen sometimes, to bring us rabbits and pheasants, and have a cup of tea.'

'We're not trespassers,' I said. 'This all belongs to my father. Pooh to the gamekeeper! Come on, let's walk along the fence. There must be a way in somewhere.'

'Oughtn't we to go back now?'

'In a minute. There's nothing to be scared of. Foxes and badgers don't attack people, you know.'

'I know that,' said Emilie. 'I'm not scared. Only we promised not to go out of sight.'

'It's my birthday, so that doesn't count. I can do what I like. That's a rule.'

She looked at me dubiously but made no further protest. We skirted the fence and suddenly a gate was there: a sturdy five-barred one with a padlock but no barbed wire.

'We can climb over,' I said triumphantly. 'I said there'd be a way in!'

Emilie was looking at something beside the gate, nailed to a sturdy post. It was a wooden board on which were black letters. I was about to say pooh to that, or something similar, when I noticed that Emilie was staring at the board, her lips moving.

She said, 'We can't go in. It says "Private. Keep out. Trespassers will be pros-e-cu-ted."' She looked at me, her eyes wide.

'We are not to go in. It says so. And that people who do will be pros-e-cu-ted. I don't know what that means. Do you?'

I didn't.

'It might mean we'll be shot,' said Emilie. 'Or even put in prison.'

The wind suddenly seemed to blow chillier. I shivered, partly with cold but also with a sudden fear. My bravado had faded away because of the message on that wooden sign.

'Well,' I said 'If you're really scared, we'd better go back to Nanny and Hobbs.'

We felt strangely subdued as we trudged back through the copse to the pony and dogcart. Whether she'd missed us or not, Nanny would not be in a good mood. And there was something else, a new thought that nagged at the back of my mind. That sign had been a meaningless jumble of letters to me. I could pick out just a short word here and there – 'will' and 'be' and 'out'. But Emilie had been able to tell me exactly what it said. She could even make out the long words. Emilie was only three days older than me, but she could already read and I could not.

CHAPTER

Emilie

I don't remember any of the time before my mother and I came to Compton Manor, not one single thing. But then I was less than a year old. Mother had told me about Bavaria, where I was born: about the beautiful forests, the mountains, the clear, pure air and the peace. She often sighed when she spoke of it, and I wondered why she had ever left. The lullabies she sang to me were always in her native tongue. She spoke it to me too, whenever we were alone in the little bedroom we shared downstairs at Compton Manor. Most of the servants lived on the attic floors, at the very top of the house, above the family and guest rooms but, because of me, Mother was given a special concession. So I grew up in the kitchen and scullery, first in a crib and then in a battered highchair, discarded from the nursery, and, later, toddling about, learning to do little jobs.

Mother considered Lady Compton to be an angel. As I grew older and could understand, she told me the story of how we had come to these shores, or some of it. Tucked up in bed together, I would lie awake and listen, although sometimes Mother was so tired after a long day's work that she would fall asleep, mid sentence.

She and my father had been childhood sweethearts. They had married and begun life in a tiny cottage in the woods, where my father worked as a forester. They were delighted to have a little daughter and looked forward to a long and happy life. But tragedy struck. A falling tree killed my father. Distraught, desolate and without income, my mother returned to her family home, where her parents ran a flourishing guest house. My mother was already a skilled pastry-cook, and was persuaded to help with the catering. Although prostrated by grief, she had no other means of support and no choice but to accept.

To the guest house came important foreign visitors: Lord and Lady Compton, the lady herself recovering from the difficult and debilitating birth of her last-born. Her doctor had prescribed a complete change of air and surroundings. They had toured several places on the Continent and were now enjoying the pure air and picturesque mountain scenery of Bavaria. They had other places to visit and stayed only two nights, but it was long enough for an attachment to form between the two young mothers, and for Lady Compton to learn some of my mother's story and be touched by it. Between that and the fact that Lord Compton heartily enjoyed my mother's baking, the idea was born that Mother and I would come to England. We would make a fresh start and my mother would work as a cook at Compton Manor; the old cook was nearing retirement. It was done. Our new home was to be a manor house in the rich, rolling, border country of Herefordshire.

'*Ach*, such an angel, she was!' my mother would reminisce fondly. '*Mein Engel*! So beautiful and gentle and kind! Such beautiful gowns, she wore! So understanding of my grief and willing to help!'

I privately thought that my mother was a big help to Lady Compton too, toiling day after day in a hot kitchen to provide meals for a family of seven, as well as a dozen or so servants and, often, numerous guests. Mother did not go much above stairs, so neither did I. Our world was the kitchen, scullery and pantries, the small bedroom we shared off the kitchen, and sometimes the kitchen garden and drying ground.

My mother was gratified when Lady Harriet and I began to be playmates. If a playtime was expected, she would dress me very carefully, make sure my pinafore was spotless, and my hair brushed and tied with a bow. My being allowed to play with her youngest daughter was another sign of Lady Compton's angelic disposition, she said. I didn't care whether Lady Compton was an angel or otherwise. Her daughter certainly was not.

I had been carefully taught to be obedient, industrious, well-mannered and, especially, never to make trouble for others. It was not usual for servants to bring up children in the kitchens of big houses, I was told. I was to be suitably appreciative of my good fortune and of those who enabled it to happen. I must be good. And I was, mostly.

Harriet herself suffered no such restrictions, although she often complained about the 'rules' she had to abide by, the burden it was to be the youngest in a large family, about Nanny's tiresome fussiness and anything else that prevented her doing exactly as she wanted. Often, she went ahead and did it anyway.

As we grew older, afternoon naps became a thing of the past. For us, anyway. Nanny usually settled herself comfortably in her armchair, with her feet on a footstool and her knitting in her lap, to 'rest her legs for a few minutes', as she said. She tended to be asleep within minutes and could be depended on not to wake for two hours at least. Harriet and I would contrive to sneak out of the nursery and go wherever our fancy took us, to poke around the stables, pick fruit in the kitchen garden, or look at the litters of piglets or new calves at the Home Farm across the fields.

'Something has happened,' Harriet told me dramatically one afternoon, when we were about seven. 'I am to have a governess! I am running wild, my mother says. I will have lessons in the morning and have to do music and needlework in the afternoons. I shall hate it!'

'You mightn't,' I said cautiously. 'You might like it. I'm going to the village school soon, Mother says. She says I must learn and not do as I like. She's got my slate and pencil, and some books, and a strap to carry everything…'

Harriet's face grew long and resentful. 'It's all right for you! You can read already! You *like* reading and writing and all those kinds of things!'

It was true. I had learned to read long before, sitting at the kitchen table, helped by my mother, Henry the footman, Ada the parlourmaid or whoever else happened to be nearby and could spare a moment. I read recipes, shopping lists, labels on bottles and everything else that had words. I found there was magic in words. I was hugely excited when Mrs Martin, the housekeeper, gave me a book of fairy stories one Christmas. I read it again and again. I could not understand Harriet's difficulty with reading; the words just seemed like a jumble of letters, she said. I tried to help her but she got bored and sometimes accused me of showing off. To be truthful, I was looking forward to school.

'I will have nobody to play with,' said Harriet mournfully. Her lower lip wobbled a little; she stuck it out in a pout and turned away. Harriet never cried. I felt a stab of remorse. I would miss her too.

I said, 'We can still play sometimes, can't we? We can still be friends.'

She whirled to face me, her eyes dark and intense. 'You must promise. Friends for ever.'

I felt the tears come to my own eyes. 'I promise.'

'We must do it properly,' she said. She was thoughtful for a moment and then said, 'There's this thing we can do to make sure we'll always be friends.' She paused. 'We each cut off a piece of our hair and plait it together. We each keep half. Then nothing can ever separate us.'

She went to Nanny's sewing basket, rummaged about, and pulled out a pair of embroidery scissors. 'These will do. I'll cut yours first.'

I felt a little uneasy as she approached, brandishing the scissors, and drew back a little.

'It won't hurt, silly,' said Harriet. 'By rights, we should each pull out a lock of hair. But I don't want to hurt you, so this will do.'

She snipped, and held up a long lock of my blonde hair. I put up my hand and felt the stubbly ends.

'No one will notice,' said Harriet briskly. 'Just pull the long bits over to hide the place. Now mine.'

She severed a long, dark lock from her own head, found some embroidery thread and tied the two tresses together. She twisted the blonde and dark to make a kind of plait. I watched as she tied the other end, then cut the plait in half and made two little bracelets by tying the end of each half together. She slipped one over her hand and held the other out to me. They were just the right size for our skinny wrists.

'To do it properly,' said Harriet, 'we would wear them all the time, for ever and ever. But Nanny or someone would be sure to make a fuss. We'll keep them secret and hide them where we keep special things. All right?'

I thought of the little box Henry had carved for me out of yew wood, with my initials on the lid.

'All right,' I said.

Nanny was stirring and we hastily jumped apart. I pulled off the bracelet of entwined hair and put it into my pinafore pocket. I knew I would treasure it for ever.

CHAPTER

Harriet

Miss Abigail Grey was my new governess. She was young, tall and slender, with shiny brunette hair and grey eyes to match her name. Her father was a clergyman, and my parents had chosen her partly because of her good upbringing and faultless manners, which virtues they no doubt hoped would rub off on me.

I soon found that Miss Grey also had a sharp mind, keen intellect and a firm hand when it came to teaching. She suffered no nonsense and expected results. She was mildly dismayed, but not deterred, when she discovered my difficulties with words and letters. She had encountered another pupil with similar difficulties, she said, and with patience and hard work the problems had been overcome. And the fact that I was quick and able with arithmetic and could remember dates and places in history and geography proved that I was not unintelligent.

So we began the laborious task of deciphering the written word. Miss Grey was patient and kind but firm, and I began to make a little progress. Most afternoons, she listened while I practised scales on the schoolroom piano, which must have been excruciating to listen to, or supervised while I sat fretting over some tray cloth to be embroidered or handkerchief to be hemmed.

Change was in the air. My father was often in London, where he stayed at his flat, and my mother was more preoccupied than ever. My sisters were restless. All three of them were now 'out' and had been presented at court in gauzy, white dresses. They had enjoyed their 'season' of parties and dances, opera and theatre visits in winter, and the country house balls, croquet games, picnics and boating parties in the summer months. These occasions were meant to bring together newly fledged young ladies and eligible young men who might be potential husbands, and would hopefully result in perfect matches. So far, my sisters had proved choosy and had avoided becoming seriously entangled, although they were all beautiful in different ways and there was never any shortage of young men coming to call. Louisa was as slim and graceful as a swan, with a chignon of blonde hair that emphasized her white, softly-rounded neck. I had seen Archie Davenport trying to nuzzle that neck as they danced at one of our summer balls, but she had expertly kept him at a distance. Caroline was dark and had long-lashed hazel eyes, and Margaret was small, dark, pretty and vivacious. Nanny was as proud of them all and my brother Hugo as though she were the mother hen who had hatched the lot. My own appearance – dark, thin and intense – caused her to sigh and remark that I must have been behind the door when looks were given out.

I cared not a jot about my looks, even as time passed and I grew older. But I was interested in the snippets of my sisters' conversations that I heard, and discussed them with Emilie when we had time to be together.

'Louisa says she couldn't possibly marry anyone without a title. And that Archie Davenport is wasting his time and might as well give up. And Caroline says she doesn't care a hoot for titles, but she won't marry a man who doesn't ride to hounds. She's really not interested in anything but horses. And Margaret isn't going to marry at all, probably, because she's going to join the Suffering Jets.'

We were in the kitchen eating the small, sweet cakes called *Magenbrot* in a rare moment when all the servants were elsewhere. They were busier than usual these days because two of them, Ada and Annie, had both left to take up other employment: Ada in a factory and Annie in a children's day nursery. There was nothing for her to do anyhow, now that I was older.

Emilie stared at me for a moment and then burst out laughing, cake crumbs spraying from her mouth.

'Oh! You mean suffragettes, not Suffering Jets!'

I was mortified at my mistake but laughed with her. 'Well, they do suffer! They chain themselves to railings and are put in prison and go on hunger strike. They have to be force-fed with those metal things that sometimes break their teeth. I heard Margaret and Caroline talking. It's all about getting equal rights for women. Votes in Parliament and all that.'

Emilie was interested. 'I think they're brave. I've read about them in the papers.'

'Have you? What papers?'

'The newspapers from upstairs. They come down here when your father has finished with them, for lighting the fires. I always try and read them first. Women are doing all kinds of new things, like riding bicycles and wearing bloomers instead of skirts.'

We giggled at that.

'Maybe we should be Suffering Jets when we're older,' said Emilie.

I wasn't sure. I liked my food and wasn't keen on the idea of going hungry and being force-fed. But riding a bicycle in bloomers might be fun. Nanny would be scandalised, but pooh to old-fashioned people like her.

It was then that I got the idea of Emilie doing her lessons with Miss Grey and me. She looked doubtful when I suggested it. I knew she loved the village school and was doing well there, learning new things all the time and hoping to go on to the grammar school. But it would be so much less tedious in the schoolroom if Emilie were there too.

I broached the subject with my mother. She was somewhat taken aback.

'I'm sure I really don't know where you get these ideas. I'll have to see. We should have to pay Miss Grey more if she were teaching two children instead of one. But Emilie is a bright girl. She might be a good influence and an inspiration. I shall have to talk to your father.'

The battle was half won. Papa was leaving more and more of the matters of the household to Mama these days. Much depended on the mood he was in when favours were asked. A cheery mood got a favourable response, but not so when Papa came home serious and depressed about the ominous things that were happening in the world. This dark mood seemed to occur more often these days.

But Mama must have caught him on a rare good day. He raised no objections to Emilie learning with me. In fact, he considered it a trifling domestic matter that, as such, barely warranted his notice. Emilie's mother was thrilled and her devotion to my mother increased a hundredfold. Janina was not at all happy about some of the children her daughter was obliged to mix with at the school. Miss Grey was keen to take up the challenge of another pupil. I was jubilant.

Emilie herself was not consulted. She was taken from the village school to join Miss Grey and me in the schoolroom at Compton Manor.

Emilie

In the beginning, I had been dismayed when I had to leave the village school and be taught in the schoolroom at Compton Manor with Harriet. I had liked the school, enjoyed the lessons and the new things I was learning, and I'd made some friends. It was pleasant, after the rarefied world of Compton Manor, to be part of a group where the children were from ordinary backgrounds. One or two of the girls had asked me to tea in their homes, which were as different as could be from the house I lived in. Here, the mother, father and children, and sometimes grandparents too, sat around a table in a small room, and talked, laughed and sometimes argued. There were no bells ringing from above, no scuttling up and down stairs, no miles of passageways and stairs to negotiate, no awareness of the privileged life of the family beyond the green baize doors. Here, we were all equal. I felt a new kind of freedom.

Then, suddenly, it all changed. I was back at Compton Manor all day again, living below stairs and spending the mornings in the schoolroom above, where all the Compton children had been taught by governesses and tutors before going on to their exclusive public schools. I disliked it intensely at first, though Harriet was delighted, and I couldn't stay resentful of her for long. After a while, I recognised the advantage of being taught in a class of only two.

'You love learning, don't you, Emilie?' Miss Grey asked on the very first day, when she saw the way my eyes went to the collection of books in the rather battered bookcase.

I nodded. Harriet scowled. She was slowly, slowly, improving her own reading but it was a laborious business. I helped her when I could but found it a tiresome and tedious task when there were scores of books waiting to be gobbled up.

'I think we'll divide ourselves up for reading lessons,' said Miss Grey. 'Harriet and I will sit over here, and perhaps you, Emilie, would like to choose a book and read by yourself in the chair by the window.'

So while the two of them sat at the table and pored over the primer that Harriet was working her way through, I escaped into the glorious realm of fiction and fantasy: tales of adventure, discovery and derring-do that transported me into magical other worlds. And it did not stop when lessons ended. Miss Grey allowed me to take books with me to read at my leisure. When I'd worked through the schoolroom ones, she brought me volumes of her own: *Jane Eyre*, *David Copperfield* and *At the back of the North Wind*. In other lessons, Harriet and I were on a par and worked together.

I adored Miss Grey. There was something about her: a quietness and confidence and a poise that owed nothing to looks or fashions. Indeed, she could not be described as a great beauty, though she was tall, slender and moved gracefully. I tried to analyse her special qualities in my own mind and could describe them only as a kind of inner light and peace.

Time passed; seasons changed. It was March and our birthdays again; we had entered our teens. Harriet, as usual, chose the way that we would celebrate and, this year, it involved her brother, Hugo. He had finished his education and was back at the manor, helping to manage the Home Farm. I saw him often out of doors, in tweeds and boots, striding about with a dog at his heels and, more often than not, a gun crooked over his arm. I thought he was wonderful: so handsome and sure of himself, like a young prince. With my head stuffed full of romantic scenes in books, I had fallen a little in love with him. My heart beat faster whenever I saw him, and if he smiled or spoke to me, I was in seventh heaven.

Harriet was pleased to have her brother home for a very different reason. He had acquired a new motor car!

'It's a Ford – a Model T!' Harriet told me importantly, bursting with excitement. 'All shiny and new. It can travel at forty miles an hour! Imagine!'

I had seen few motors as I did not go to any large towns or cities, except once when I had a raging toothache and was taken to a dentist. There was a motor in the garage at Compton Manor, a Rolls Royce Silver Ghost, I had been told, in which the chauffeur Beddows sometimes drove Lord and Lady Compton to some function or other. Harriet had never ridden in it; she had been told, much to her indignation, that children tended to leave sticky finger marks on the shiny surfaces. Any outings she had, which I sometimes shared with her, were in the carriage, behind well-groomed horses, now that we were too big to squeeze into the dogcart.

'Papa was so against Hugo having a fast motor,' said Harriet. 'He really is so old-fashioned, you wouldn't believe. But Hugo persuaded Mama, and Mama persuaded Papa.' She pulled a face. 'Hugo is her golden boy, you know. She can deny him nothing. Anyway, the car is coming here, and I am going to ride in it!'

I looked at her doubtfully. 'Will it be safe, going so fast?'

'Oh, yes! Hugo has learnt to drive already. And even if it isn't quite safe, think what fun it will be, going like the wind! We shall enjoy it, you'll see!'

'We?'

'Yes. I've made Hugo promise to take us out in it for our birthday treat! Mama says Miss Grey must come too. Thankfully, it won't be Nanny!'

Nanny barely stirred from the nursery these days.

I didn't know what to think. A motor car: a mechanical, wheeled, metal conveyance that was powered by an engine. And with Hugo driving! I was panic-stricken and wildly excited in equal measure.

The day came, a dull, chilly afternoon, and we joined Miss Grey on the wide sweep of gravel at the front of the house. Hugo fetched the car, with a great deal of noise from the motor and a crunch of wheels on gravel as he cruised, with a proud grin, up to the door. It was splendid: shiny, cherry red, picked out in black, and with seats upholstered in gleaming leather, two in front and two smaller ones at the back. Hugo leaped out and opened the front passenger door with a little bow, motioning Miss Grey to get in. 'Step in, Miss Grey – or may I call you Abigail?' he asked, with that heart-stopping smile of his.

She gave him a level look from her grey eyes and said coolly, 'Miss Grey will be appropriate, I think. Thank you.'

He grinned. From what I had read in romantic novels, I would have said he was lightly flirting with her. The ladies in the stories were usually foolish creatures who reacted by becoming coy, blushing prettily or lowering their eyes. Miss Grey did none of these things but, if anything, seemed a little more aloof than usual. She was looking rather pretty in a neat green suit and a peplum jacket, her wide hat covered with a gauzy scarf.

'Righto, then! Little girls in the back,' said Hugo. We climbed in; the car started with a jerk and a strong smell of petrol, and we were off down the drive, the trees and grass of the park flashing by at an alarming rate. Hugo seemed rather an erratic driver; I wished for a slower pace, although Harriet loved the speed and urged him to go quicker. He laughed and did so, with a sideways glance at Miss Grey to see if she was impressed. She sat with her kid-gloved hands in her lap, as composed as ever. If she was nervous, she did not show it. I clutched the edges of the seat and prayed that there wouldn't be an accident. We drove around the park and into the village, where Hugo tooted the horn and anyone in the street smartly got out of the way. I saw a couple of boys I'd been at school with, their mouths open. Then we were through the village and out into the countryside, bare fields on either side.

'Spiffing, isn't it?' said Hugo above the noise of the engine.

Harriet was loving it all, her eyes sparkling and her hair escaping her hat. 'Oh, I want to learn to drive!' she said.

'In a year or two maybe, Shrimp,' said Hugo. 'Not sure whether there are any women drivers, though.'

'I could be the first,' said Harriet.

We took a tour on the road that circled the big wood and then returned through the village, into the Compton parkland and back to the house, where we pulled up, with a couple of sharp toots of the horn and a rather sudden jerk. I found that I was trembling, and mightily relieved to be back safely. Hugo again made a great show of handing Miss Grey out of the car.

'Thank you,' she said calmly, gathering her skirts together.

'My pleasure,' he said with a little bow. 'Until next time, then.'

Miss Grey didn't reply to that. She said, 'Come, girls,' and led us inside, where Harriet ran upstairs, cheeks glowing, to change before tea in the drawing room. I took the back passageway to the busy kitchen.

CHAPTER

Seven

Harriet

That summer was fun. The weather was beautiful: lots of long days full of sunshine, week after week, as though it would never end. My father was still away a great deal, involved in the business and political worlds of which I knew little and understood less. When he was home, he sometimes tried to explain to the rest of us the state of the world, especially our country, round the dinner table. There was the problem of the demand for Home Rule in Ireland, he said. There was trouble with factory workers striking for more pay, and there were more and more women signing up to do men's work, which would undoubtedly cause more problems.

'Yes, it's a great inconvenience,' sighed my mother. 'Dora has given notice. She wants to leave to go to work in a sweet factory. That means Hannah will have to look after me. But her hands are so rough that they tug my hair and snag my silk stockings.'

Margaret threw a challenging look at her across the table. 'Maybe the days are coming when you will have to dress yourself and do your own hair, Mother.'

Mama gave her a look of reproach. 'You have such strange ideas, Margaret. I can't think that going to those suffrage meetings does you any good at all. They have quite changed you.'

Margaret tossed her head. 'Good! It's time for change. Time for women to speak up and claim their dues. Good for Dora, and all the others. I wish them well.'

My father frowned at her. 'Be careful, Margaret. Change is not always for the better. And if our people continue to leave at this rate, how will we keep up this house and estate? Are you prepared to rise at dawn to clean grates and lay fires? Is your mother to cook for us? Will Hugo clean out the pigsties, groom the horses and dig the vegetable plot?'

Hugo gave a snort of laughter, helping himself to another slice of toast. 'Can't see that happening, although I might polish up the Ford if Beddows decides to take off.'

I couldn't help grinning myself. A picture of my sisters, in grubby pinafores, on their hands and knees scrubbing floors had come into my mind, along with the even less likely one of my mother peeling potatoes and gutting a rabbit, as I had watched Cook – Janina – do. The conversation ended when Dawkins came in with coffee and it was time for Mama and the girls to take themselves to the drawing room, while Papa and Hugo lingered over cigars. For me, it meant bedtime, although I was fast outgrowing the nursery routines.

I didn't waste much time pondering political and social problems. We had fun that summer. There were outings and excursions, croquet parties on the lawn and picnics by the lake. I had several weeks of glorious freedom from lessons, while Miss Grey went home to her father's rectory.

Just before the freedom began, all of us at Compton decamped to the seaside for the day, including the servants, who travelled in a chattering, excited group by train. Mama, Papa and my sisters were driven in the Silver Ghost, and a few of us squeezed into Hugo's car, including me, by reason of earnest pleading, Emilie, who was nervous but came to keep me company and Miss Grey, who had not yet left for her summer break. Miss Grey seemed displeased with the arrangement but could not leave her charges unchaperoned, and I loved the car so much that I would not even consider going on the train with the others.

'Harriet, perhaps you would like to ride in front,' she said as we were about to embark. This suggestion brought a cloud to Hugo's face. He said, 'Well, I'd rather sit beside you, Abigail. Hattie does chatter so.' But Miss Grey only pursed her lips at the disrespectful use of her Christian name and climbed into the back seat with Emilie. I got in beside Hugo, delighted to have a clear view of the road ahead and everything we passed. At Hugo's request, I did not chatter. In any case, he did all the talking, throwing remarks over his shoulder to Miss Grey. Sometimes he'd turn his head to look at her, once even swerving across the road when he lost concentration for a second. She and Emilie both gasped. Miss Grey said, 'Please do keep your attention on the road.'

It seemed to make him even more talkative, even a little saucy, I thought, because somehow his remarks turned to bathing in the sea, bathing costumes and her opinion of mixed bathing. Miss Grey gave short answers. For someone who talked all the time in the schoolroom, she had become very silent. I put it down to nerves.

For me, the journey was over too soon. The countryside had flashed by in a haze of summer foliage, wild roses in the hedgerows, fleeting scents of honeysuckle and sunshine dappled through leaves. Then, at the end, we were tumbling out of the Ford to join the others.

The day passed in a heady mix of sea, sand and sunshine. We changed into our bathing costumes and paddled in the waves curling and crashing to the shore. Neither Emilie nor I could swim, but we lay down in shallow water and pretended, flapping our arms and kicking our legs, cumbered by the thick serge of our costumes. We picnicked from several large hampers carried down by the servants, and giggled at Mrs Martin and Cook, who had hitched up their skirts and were dabbling their feet in the water.

'Salt water does wonders for the corns and bunions,' we heard Mrs Martin remark.

Miss Grey sat on a folding chair, fully clothed in a pretty light summer blouse and skirt. After a while, Hugo went and stretched out on the sand beside her. Emilie and I were too engrossed building sandcastles and ornamenting them with shells to bother listening to their talk, but, after a while, I saw that Miss Grey had got up and gone to sit next to Polly and Hannah, the kitchen maids. It struck me as rather strange; usually, she did not mix much with the servants.

On the way home, Miss Grey took the train with the others and, despite my protests, I was obliged to ride with Mama and Papa in the Rolls Royce, while my sisters went with Hugo in his car. I did not know whose idea this was, but I was put out. A fast, thrilling ride home in Hugo's car would have been the perfect end to a perfect day.

CHAPTER

Emilie

From my very earliest days, my mother had instilled in me the importance of good manners. I learned to be polite to all, respect my elders (which meant anyone older than I was) and my betters (which meant the family above stairs and everyone of their class). If I transgressed, talked back when reprimanded or made a remark or observation – often quite innocently on my part – that was deemed rude or impertinent, I would be chastised: a smack on the bottom when I was small; a lecture and icy disapproval as I grew older. I was not keen on any of these punishments; indeed, I believe, I was, by nature, a well-mannered child and so was not often corrected.

I would never have dreamed of being impolite to Lord and Lady Compton, any of the family, Nanny, Miss Grey or anyone else in the household. I couldn't imagine myself eavesdropping on a private conversation, lurking around corners, listening outside doors or at keyholes to hear the talk within.

Harriet had none of my scruples. She unashamedly hung about when grown-ups talked, and eavesdropped, concealing herself behind curtains or pieces of furniture in order to overhear interesting conversations. When I remonstrated with her, she said, 'Well, I have to, don't I? No one ever tells me a thing. I'd be completely ignorant of anything going on in this house if I didn't find out for myself.'

Whether this was true or one of her exaggerations, I have no idea. It didn't stop her anyway, which made it all the stranger that it was I, and not Harriet, who heard the exchange between Hugo and Miss Grey on the night of the seaside excursion.

It had been a long day and everyone was tired. In the kitchen, there were picnic baskets to unpack, a light supper for the family to be prepared and the usual preparations to be made for the next morning. Despite the clothing I'd worn, my fair skin had caught the sun and turned it pink wherever it was exposed. My mother said she'd fetch some camomile to soothe the sunburn when she had a minute.

Harriet came into the kitchen looking for me. She took one look at the weary, harassed faces and whispered to me, 'Come on, let's get out of here.'

We went out at the back door and wandered into the kitchen garden. From there, we took the path to the rose arbour at the side that overlooked the lawns sweeping right round the house, beyond the gravel driveway. It wasn't quite dark, the evenings were still long, but the moon was showing itself half-full, and the bushes and trees were in deep shadow and seemed mysterious. Although it had been a hot, dry day, the gardens had been well-watered and the air was full of the sweetness of roses and night-scented stocks. We went into the rose arbour and sat on the swing seat, rocking to and fro gently, enjoying the peace.

'Is your sunburn sore?' asked Harriet. She peered at me through the dimness. 'I'm sure you're getting pinker!'

I touched my arm and winced. 'It is a bit. I wish I'd stayed in the shade.'

Harriet yawned. 'Me, I don't burn. I just tan. Mama and the girls think it's dreadful and that I look like a gypsy. They say I'll never find anyone to marry me. As though I care!'

We swung in silence for a few minutes, watching as the dusk deepened and as bats began to swoop and flitter in search of insects, our young ears able to hear their high-pitched squeaks.

Then Harriet said, 'Do you suppose we shall marry? One day?'

I hadn't given marriage much thought. All my romantic notions so far had been centred on Hugo, but I'd never thought of marrying him. I knew it would never happen. His wife would be a daughter of an upper-class landowner.

I sighed. 'I suppose so. It's what girls do, isn't it?'

'I shan't,' declared Harriet. 'Never! I want to do something else with my life, have adventures, see other places. You and I could travel together. We're forever sisters, after all.' She thought a little longer, then added, 'If I do marry, it won't be until I'm about thirty-five.'

Thirty-five seemed a lifetime away. Harriet yawned again. 'I'm tired. I'm going in to bed now. Are you coming?'

'In a minute,' I said. I was enjoying the cooler air on my warm skin and the quiet after the bustle of the day. I sat silently for a few minutes after she'd gone.

A voice spoke suddenly, close at hand. I jumped; I hadn't heard anyone approach.

'Ah, there you are! I've been looking all over for you.'

Hugo! I had been thinking of him and now he was here! For a moment, I thought he was talking to me and my heart began to pound. But another voice answered, the low, clear voice of Miss Grey, sounding unusually startled. 'Oh! I – I was just getting some air. I didn't know you were here.'

He laughed. 'It's fate, then. You've been avoiding me all day. Now I can have you all to myself.'

She seemed flustered, another unusual circumstance. 'I have to go back.'

'Not yet. Stay and talk to me. Let's sit in the arbour for a bit.'

My heart gave a great leap. They were coming here! I'd be discovered listening – eavesdropping!

But Miss Grey said, 'No, Hugo. Please – you mustn't go on like this—'

'Why not? Don't you know I'm crazy about you? I think you like me too.' She didn't reply. He went on. 'You do like me, don't you? I can tell, you know. I can always tell when a girl likes me.'

'I'm not a girl. I'm older than you by at least two years. And besides—'

'Besides what? That you're a prim and proper clergyman's daughter? You never flirt or enjoy yourself. Are you saving yourself for Mr Perfect?'

There was a firmness to Miss Grey's voice now that I hadn't heard before. 'It's nothing to do with being a clergyman's daughter. My faith is my own. I am a follower of Christ and I obey his commands. And you're right, I don't believe in light flirtations.'

'All right then, marry me! I mean it. I'm serious.'

'Don't be ridiculous! I'm going inside now.'

'Give me a kiss first!'

'No. Goodnight.'

I heard the rustle of her skirts and light footsteps on the gravel as she walked away. He called after her, a note of desperation in his voice. 'There's a war coming and I'm applying for a commission. I might be killed in battle. Then you'd be sorry!'

Even to my ears, this sounded childish and petulant. Miss Grey must have thought so too, for there was no reply, just the gentle closing of the front door. Hugo swore and kicked something; it must have been hard, maybe one of the large stones bordering the path, because he gave a yelp of pain and swore again. I heard him muttering as he walked away, and then the front door closed again but not quite so gently; this time it was slammed.

I had been holding my breath and let it out in a long sigh. My skin was prickling, and not just with sunburn. My mind was a jumble of thoughts and emotions. I got up and stretched my cramped limbs. For a moment, I debated going to see whether Harriet was still up and discussing with her what I'd heard. But I thought it wasn't something to gossip and giggle over. Forever sisters or not, this was not a conversation I was going to share with her.

CHAPTER

Harriet

We had a month of glorious freedom, Emilie and I: no lessons and four weeks of long summer days that seemed as though they would never end. Emilie had jobs to do in the kitchen, but as soon as she was free, we would take off to the woods, river, parkland or wherever our fancy led us. I had a pony and Emilie had learned to ride too. It was frustrating, though, that there weren't two ponies so that we could ride together.

We had picnics by the river, pretended that we were explorers in the Amazon basin, built huts out of hazel boughs and moss, and 'lived off the land' or, in other words, stole ripe raspberries, plums and peaches from the kitchen garden when the gardener was not about. We devoured them, giggling, in the shade of the rose arbour. My tan deepened and even Emilie's fair skin took on a delicate hint of brown. Our bare legs had scratches from brambles and sometimes itchy heat lumps. Nanny scolded when she noticed but, these days, she wasn't noticing as much as she once had. Mama sighed and wondered whether she would ever make a lady of me.

And then the blow fell. Miss Grey would not be coming back. Although the end of her month's holiday was near, she would not be returning to Compton Manor. Emilie and I were both dismayed. We had regretted the coming end of our freedom but looked forward to seeing Miss Grey again. Emilie, in particular, was downcast; she and Miss Grey were both bookish and often discussed what they'd read and what they'd like to read. I had to admit that, but for Miss Grey, I would probably still be struggling to read at all. I didn't enjoy books as they did, but she made every lesson interesting and left me wanting to learn more. Now, Mama told me, my parents would be looking for a good boarding school for me.

'But why?' I wailed. 'We were fine as we were. Why can't she come back?'

Mother pursed her lips and told me I must not ask questions about matters that did not concern me.

'But it does concern me!' I said and, like a sulky child, aimed a kick at the leg of the dining table. 'I am the one it concerns most, I should think!'

My mother was, unlike her, standing firm in the face of my childish tantrums. 'You are not the centre of the universe, Harriet, though you may choose to think so. It was a mutual decision and the reasons do not concern you. You are behaving like a spoilt child, so I suggest you go to your room and regain your composure before it's time for dinner, or you will be taking yours in the nursery with Nanny.'

Smarting, I retreated upstairs but, after ten minutes of fuming in my room, I sneaked down the back stairs and through the green baize doors. A hubbub of talk died away as I entered the kitchen. I grabbed Emilie, who was polishing silver at the big table, and dragged her out into the kitchen garden. Emilie was looking uneasy, as though she knew something that I didn't.

'What is going on?' I demanded. 'Why is Miss Grey going? Why is everything changing?'

Emilie broke off a piece of lavender and sniffed it. 'Haven't they told you?'

'No! Told me what?'

'Well, about Miss Grey and why she won't be back. It's all the talk in the kitchen.' She twirled a strand of her blonde hair and looked embarrassed. 'It's... it's to do with Hugo.'

'Hugo?' I stared at her, puzzled.

'Yes. They're saying that there was something going on between them. Something improper.'

I laughed. 'That's just Hugo! He's like that with lots of girls, if they're pretty. Margaret says he's a natural flirt. Miss Grey didn't need to worry about that.'

Emilie looked embarrassed again. 'Well, they're saying that your mother and father – that is, Lord and Lady Compton – consider that it's Miss Grey's fault, that she was making a play for him, because he's the heir and all that, and that a stop had to be put to it.'

'What nonsense!' I said. 'Miss Grey never made a play for him, whatever that means. She didn't like him much, I thought. It wasn't her fault. I shall tell Mama and Papa!'

'Don't!' said Emilie. 'I'll be in trouble for gossiping.'

'Well, it's not fair, and I want Miss Grey back,' I said.

'She won't come,' said Emilie. 'She's staying at home to help her father because her mother is unwell. Didn't they tell you that?'

'They never tell me anything,' I said bitterly. 'Well, if they try to send me to some stupid school, I won't go. I'll run away. We'll both run away.'

'I don't want to,' said Emilie. She stared at me, a determined look I hadn't seen before in her blue eyes. I had a sudden feeling of panic, of events going too quickly for me, of slipping beyond my control.

I said, 'You have to. We've got to stick together. We're forever sisters, remember?'

She said nothing. I looked at her, in her print dress, pinafore and black stockings. I realised how tall she had grown, almost a head taller than me. We were fourteen years old; we would soon be wearing long skirts and putting our hair up. We would be young women and not children any more.

'Haven't you noticed,' she said, 'that there is something going on, something big? I don't mean Miss Grey and Hugo, although I've noticed he's been in a mood lately, banging doors and frowning all the time and shouting at the dogs.'

I stared at her. I had vaguely noticed Hugo's moodiness, now that she mentioned it. What an observant creature she was.

'What do you mean, something big?'

She shrugged. 'Something to do with politics and other countries. I've read bits in the papers, but everyone else is grabbing them now before I get a chance. There's trouble coming.'

'What kind of trouble?'

We were interrupted by Emilie's mother coming to the kitchen door and calling her. '*Ach*, there you are! Come back and finish the job you were doing. And Lady Harriet, I believe your sister is looking for you.'

There was no more conversation between us that day. But, the next morning, we all learned what the trouble was. Our country was at war.

Harriet

I knew what war was, of course. It was two nations fighting each other over land or to gain independence or some such. In our history lessons with Miss Grey, we had studied the Boer War, the Crimean War and so on. But why our own nation should be at war now I just could not understand, and I became more confused than ever when I asked the adults in my family. This war had started because some archduke had been shot dead in a European country, I was told, though why that had anything to do with us in England I couldn't comprehend at all. But it had.

Everyone went about with serious faces. My father immediately caught a train to London to see to his business concerns and political interests, which would all be affected. My mother, my sisters and Hugo had serious discussions around the dining table, which often turned into heated arguments, mostly between Margaret and Hugo. The servants huddled in little groups, and there was a strange atmosphere in the kitchen, with people falling silent whenever Emilie and I were around. I tried hard to overhear their conversations, but everyone exchanged meaningful looks and wouldn't even answer my questions.

Then one evening, when my father had returned, I arrived at the door of the small sitting room where he and my mother were seated after dinner. They were talking so intensely that they did not notice me at first.

'I can't believe you're telling me I should let her go,' said my mother, in a voice so plaintive that she sounded near to tears. 'Not Janina. Not after all these years! She has been so good, so devoted. She is spotlessly clean, hardworking, loyal, and I've never seen such an excellent cook. My table is the envy of the county.'

'Yes, yes. I know all that!' my father said testily. 'I shall miss her cooking too, believe me. But there are more important issues than successful dinner parties to consider now. We are at war, Sophia. Feelings are running high. Aliens are being deported already, you know. Sent home to Germany. I cannot appear unpatriotic. You must understand that. Our personal feelings must be put aside in the interests of our country.'

He had raised his voice and now paused. 'Harbouring enemy aliens under our roof would not be regarded as patriotic. You must see that. They have to go – she and the girl.'

'Couldn't we just wait a little and see how matters turn out?' said my mother, pleading. 'The war may be over very soon, then all will be as usual, and we can live normally again. We may come to regret any hasty action.'

Papa cleared his throat and muttered. He was usually soft with Mama when she pleaded. He cleared his throat again. 'We'll leave it, just for a while. But I think they should change their names. Schmidt is so obvious.'

My mother seized on this eagerly. 'Yes, yes. I'll speak to Cook! She could be Janet. Or Janice. And Emilie would just need to change the spelling of her name.'

My heart was thumping so fast that I thought they must surely hear. They were talking about Cook: Janina, Emilie's mother. They were even thinking of sending her away – Emilie too – or changing their names. All because of the war and because they were German.

I must have made a sound because they turned and saw me standing in the doorway.

'Harriet,' said my mother irritably. 'Must you creep about listening to private conversations?'

'I couldn't help it,' I said. And then a sob came into my throat and I threw all caution to the winds. 'Why should they change their names?' I demanded. 'Why must everything change? I hate the war! And if you send them away, I will hate you too!'

43

And then I turned and headed for the privacy of my room. I hardly ever cried, but I found that tears were streaming down my face.

*

Nobody talked of anything but the war, above or below stairs. The initial shock soon gave way to something close to feelings of excitement and anticipation. As well as the regular soldiers being mobilised, scores of ordinary lads were signing up to join the army and take part in what they believed would be a big adventure. On a visit to the village with Margaret, I saw a line of young men queuing to get into the village hall. They were laughing, making jokes and shoving one another as though they were on a jolly day out.

'What are they doing?' I asked. 'Why are they going there?'

'It's a makeshift recruitment centre,' said my sister. 'They're signing up.'

'Signing up?' I was puzzled.

'Yes, to go and fight in France, push back the invaders,' she said. Her eyes were sparkling; she seemed almost as excited as the young men. 'Our brave lads are going to do their duty, and I wish them all the luck in the world.'

I looked at her. 'Would you go if you were a man?'

She laughed. 'Wouldn't I just! But there might be something, even for girls like me...'

She didn't go on but hurried across the street to post our letters, smiling and nodding at some of the lads, who recognised her and grinned broadly, doffing their caps. It seemed almost like a public holiday.

I didn't know what Margaret meant. Was it something to do with the Suffering Jets? But she was in too much of a hurry to answer any more of my questions. I wondered if Hugo would enlist, but I couldn't see him joining that queue of local men and farm hands.

I asked Mama about it later that evening, when my father and Hugo were smoking their cigars in the dining room. A shadow flitted over her face.

'He is talking about applying for a commission and joining your father's old regiment,' she said. She bit her lip. 'They say it will all be over by

Christmas, but I'm not so sure. Once these conflicts begin, there's no knowing...'

I could guess how hard it would be for her if her precious only son had to go off to war. I was surprised to hear from kitchen gossip that many women were actively encouraging their men to join the army and were full of pride when they did. A huge wave of patriotism was sweeping the land, affecting even our sheltered lives at Compton Manor. And there was something else; something that seemed to swirl around in the air: a strange feeling of unease that I couldn't quite place but that gave me a queasy feeling in my stomach, as though something else were going to happen.

I found out the cause on an evening when my father returned home from one of his trips to London.

Part Two
Emilie

CHAPTER

Eleven

Up until that summer, I'd been a child; after that time, I never felt like a child again. It was as though, with the passing of those long, golden days, a greyness and a gloom came that held an unknown and terrible menace.

I should have been aware of what was to come, and maybe I was but chose to close my eyes to it. I read the newspapers or as much of them as I could before they were scrunched up and used to start a fire in one of the many fireplaces. There had been rumblings and rumours in political circles for a long time, not that politics or even the possibility of trouble in Europe interested me much. But now it was here, in our own midst. People even looked different, preoccupied, anxious or apprehensive, or just bewildered. Some seemed exhilarated.

Henry came bursting in one morning as preparations for lunch were under way.

'I've signed up!'

Everyone looked at him: Mother, up to her wrists in flour and butter for pie pastry, and Polly with a tray of cups and saucers from elevenses upstairs; Mrs Martin, who had been frowning at the day's menus, peered at him over her reading glasses. I had been scraping carrots with a book propped open in front of me, a habit Mrs Martin tut-tutted over but indulged.

'I'm off!' said Henry, a big grin on his freckled face. 'Took the king's shilling. I'm going for training in a couple of weeks! Can't wait! So it'll be goodbye to all this!'

He waved his hand dismissively at the organised clutter of the kitchen.

'Can you do it – just like that?' asked Polly uncertainly. I had thought that she was a little sweet on Henry, although he'd never seemed to notice her much. She put down her tray of china and covered her mouth with her hand.

'I can and I have,' said Henry jauntily, taking off his jacket and rolling up his sleeves. 'So you won't be seeing me for a while. It'll be cheerio and all that.'

'Well, we're seeing you now, so I'd be glad if you'd favour us with a little work while you're here,' said Mrs Martin tartly.

Polly sighed and began to pile cups into the sink.

When I questioned Mother, in private, she refused to speak about the situation.

'But we have family still in Germany,' I said.

'*Ach*, they are in the country. The war will be nothing to do with them,' said Mother dismissively. She chose not to say any more.

But there were things that could not be ignored. Now that Miss Grey no longer taught Harriet and me, I had been sent back to the village school. I protested vehemently. 'I am fourteen already! That is school-leaving age. The school will be full of younger children. I will learn nothing there!'

'Just for a while,' said Mother. 'You must keep up with your studies, and then I hope you will win a scholarship to the grammar school. You have been a little spoiled here, I think. You must go.'

So to the village school I went, fuming, and sat with the other boys and girls my age, whom, I soon learned, I had far outstripped in almost everything. And there was something else. From the very first day, I sensed a hostility, not just from the pupils but from the teachers too. Miss Cole was particularly cold towards me.

'You may have been privately educated, Emilie, but, believe me, you have a lot to learn,' she told me, when she had summed up my education to date. 'You will receive no special treatment here, I assure you.'

I did receive special treatment but not of the kind she meant. A girl pushed me against a doorpost, as we entered a room together, and then said spitefully, 'Oh, I'm *so* sorry!'

I would find my neatly piled books higgledy-piggledy if I'd left them for a few minutes, and I was always last to be picked in any team game in the playground. Girls looked at me, whispered behind their hands and giggled.

At first, I thought it was because I'd come from Compton Manor and I'd had a governess and was clever. I could deal with that. But one day my eyes were opened to the truth. A boy my age suddenly confronted me in the schoolyard and spat in the dust at my feet. I stared at him, astonished. 'Why did you do that?'

He sneered and didn't reply, but another, bolder, lad came forward and said, 'Because you're a dirty rotten Hun, that's why! My brother and *his* brother,' he indicated the boy who had spat, 'they're going over to thrash the living daylights out of you Hun. You're the enemy and we hate you!'

I went home in tears, feeling my world suddenly crumbling about me. I thought my mother would insist that I go back to school and face whatever might come. But she did not. She was not angry, but she had a look I'd never seen on her face before. It was naked fear.

She took me by the shoulders. 'Emilie, you need not go back there. Everything is changing, and maybe for us they will change most of all. Be prepared. Pray God we can get through this storm.'

I was shaken and scared by her vehemence. 'But, Mother, we are not the enemy! Lord and Lady Compton know that. They will take care of us.'

'They may not be able to,' she said grimly. 'Feelings run high in time of war.'

She hesitated. 'I wasn't going to tell you this but, yesterday, the man in the baker's refused to serve me.' She lowered her voice, though we were in our bedroom and no one could hear. 'And even here, in this house, there's difficulty with the other servants. Not all but some. They look at me differently. Suspiciously.'

I had noticed a coolness in the usual, happy-go-lucky atmosphere of the kitchen, but hadn't connected it with us at all, thinking that the war was casting a blight over everything.

'I even heard someone muttering about German spies,' she said. There was a note of real fear in her voice. I hugged her, my capable, calm mother who could manage everything. Seeing her like this scared me.

'Mother, it will be all right.'

She nodded and pulled herself together. '*Ach*, you're a good girl. As long as we have each other, *Liebchen*.'

A few days later came another bombshell. Mother was called to speak to Lord and Lady Compton in private, upstairs. Those in the kitchen looked at one another and there were a few meaningful nods. But I was there, and nothing was said. Mrs Martin gave the others a frosty look and came over to put her arm around me. 'Don't you fret, my love. It's probably nothing much.'

But I knew it wasn't nothing. Wild fancies chased themselves through my mind. Were we to be sent away? Where would we go? Why did everyone suddenly hate us just because of the country we were born in?

By the time Mother came back I had worked myself into a state of panic. Her eyes were red and her usually rosy cheeks paler than normal. I feared the worst. She took my hand and pulled me into the passage and away from curious eyes.

'Are we to leave?' I asked fearfully.

She shook her head. '*Nein, nein*. We stay.' Mother sometimes forgot her careful English when she was agitated. 'We stay, at least for now. They are kindness itself. My lady is an angel, as I have always said. But we change our names, to sound more English. I will be Janet; you, Emily, with the English spelling. You will be Emily Smith.'

CHAPTER

Twelve

It was a long and strange time, that autumn and winter, with everything at Compton Manor the same and yet changed. Henry and a number of other young men from the village and farms had joined up, eager for a change and a taste of adventure. There had been great goings-on when a group of them marched away to begin their training, with the Compton Manor staff given the afternoon off to watch the parade, a sense of the festive in the air.

'You'd think it was some jolly junket going on over there, not a war,' muttered Mrs Martin darkly, coming into the kitchen in her hat and coat, ready to join the bystanders. 'I have to say, I'm glad I have no sons to be waving off to who knows what.'

Mrs Martin's views were not shared by everyone. There was a poster in the village shop that featured a mother, a young woman and a boy watching soldiers marching off. Its caption said, 'Women of Britain say – "Go!"' Pictures of Lord Kitchener were everywhere, in which he stared straight ahead, pointing his finger. Beneath this intimidating image was a bold statement: 'Your country needs YOU!'

Certainly, a kind of fever seemed to have gripped the nation and spread like wildfire to every town, village and hamlet.

Mother was uncomfortable with the whole thing. 'I can't help thinking that it is us, our country, that they are going to fight,' she told me as we got our coats from the bedroom. 'All this rejoicing and boasting, it is for the defeat of our people.'

But we went, because it would have looked strange not to, and these days we were careful not to draw attention to ourselves. We were now Janet and Emily Smith if anyone asked.

Harriet went to the parade with her sisters but contrived to slip away to join me and the rest of the staff. The village street seemed to be a mass of shifting, excited bodies in carnival mood; Union Jacks were fluttering and tongues chattering. Harriet and I worked our way through the crowd until we were near the front.

We hadn't long to wait. We could hear the parade approaching, accompanied by the local brass band, playing the songs that had sprung into popularity, such as 'It's a Long Way to Tipperary' and other rousing marching songs. Then round the corner came the band, instruments gleaming in the autumn sun, followed by a marching column of khaki-clad young men. They were all kitted out in their brand-new uniform tunics and trousers of thick-looking material and boots. Bandages, which I was told were called puttees, were wound round their legs to the knees. Metal helmets and guns were slung over their shoulders. All of them had the same kind of look: proud, excited; maybe a touch unsure of their ability to march in time to the beat, but eager and showing off a little for the benefit of the onlookers. They were young and fresh-faced, strong and fit from labouring at farm work, and tanned from the long, hot summer. Some of them I'd known from my earlier years in school or seen about the village. And there were also faces I knew well: Henry and Ben, the gardener's boy, and lads from the Home Farm.

I felt a sudden lump come into my throat. Beside me, Polly was sniffling into her handkerchief, but she had a Michaelmas daisy in her hand and threw it out to Henry as he went by. He caught it, turned his head and waved his salute to the group of us from the manor, his freckled face split by a big grin. Polly looked as though she didn't know whether to laugh or cry, so did both.

Others were cheering and throwing flowers or even darting out and pressing them into the hands of the proud, young soldiers. Children were running alongside to keep pace with the marching ranks. Then I saw a scuffle going on a little distance ahead. Necks craned to see what was happening. I saw a flurry of something white float into the air.

Harriet's sharp eyes hadn't missed a thing. 'They're white feathers,' she said. 'They're handing out white feathers to young men not in uniform.'

I followed her gaze and could see a group of young women, strangers to our village, moving among the crowd, handing out the feathers to men. Some took them, looking blank and surprised or even puzzled; others refused and ducked their heads, turning away in embarrassment.

I was perplexed. 'What are they doing?'

'It's a sign of cowardice,' said Harriet. 'Margaret told me. Getting a white feather is meant to shame them into enlisting.'

The men in the crowd did look ashamed, shuffling their feet awkwardly as the detachment marched away round the bend by the church, the beat of the band fading away in the distance. I noticed Margaret talking to some of the girls who had been giving out the white feathers.

'Do the Suffering Jets think everyone should join up?' I asked.

'Not sure,' said Harriet. 'Margaret's up to something though. She's behaving mysteriously, as if there's a plot in the air.'

The whole thing – the parade, the cheering, the flowers, the white feathers – had given me an odd feeling. I was not a part of any of this, and yet I was here. I had been called an enemy, and yet this place and this way of life were all I knew.

The crowd was dispersing; the people were animated and chattering. Harriet's eyes were sparkling.

'Let's not go home yet,' she said. 'They won't notice. Let's walk about the village and listen to what everyone is saying.' She peered at me. 'You're awfully quiet. Aren't you enjoying it? Oh, I forgot! You're not on our side, are you? You're an alien.'

She meant it lightly, teasingly, and linked her arm in mine as she spoke. But her words struck home. I wanted suddenly to be far away from this scene, this fevered madness or so it seemed. I shivered in spite of the warm afternoon, and wanted nothing more than to go home, pick up an engrossing book and retreat to another, saner, world.

*

They said it would all be over by Christmas, but they were wrong. By Christmas, more men had been deployed and were engaged in fierce combat in Belgium and France, so we learned. I had given up reading the newspapers. Every day there were lists of those who had died in battle and those who had been wounded. Mrs Martin would read them, shed a tear and murmur, 'Those poor, brave boys!'

Mother and I did not join in discussions of the war. I continued to feel a cool distance between us and the rest of the staff. It seemed almost as though they blamed us for those lists of dead young men. Sometimes I felt a twinge of resentment, thinking that there were surely such lists in our country too. But, mostly, I felt a huge sadness.

Christmas was a more sombre occasion than the lavish celebrations of the past. Food was still plentiful, but Lady Compton made a big issue of being what she called 'frugal', which meant cutting back on the geese, beef, mutton and game that would usually be consumed, and 'making do' with a goose and perhaps a ham. Mother was instructed to eke out the rich ingredients of cakes, puddings and pies with plainer stuff. In other words, she was to use slightly less fruit, butter and sugar, and make fewer rich sauces.

Lady Compton organised packages of 'home comforts' for the boys on the front line. The winter was setting in and they must be in need of warm socks, mufflers and gloves. She cut down on the Christmas boxes for the staff, decreeing that they should forego their annual gift of cloth for uniforms and make do with the ones they had for another year. She herself, she said, would be ordering no new gowns.

It was not the happiest Christmas. But one thing, for me, stood out like the gleam of gold. A few days after the festive season, newspapers carried reports of a strange happening in the front-line trenches. On Christmas Eve, the guns had fallen silent and then a soldier, a German, began to sing 'Silent Night' in a beautiful tenor voice. Others joined in. Then, like a miracle, the British had joined in too. Voices rose from both lines of trenches into the cold wintry air. And on Christmas Day, one of the soldiers – whether German or British, I don't know – scrambled out of his trench, and others joined him from both sides. They met in no man's land, laughed and joked, and exchanged little gifts from home. They even found a football and enjoyed an impromptu match. No guns were fired all that day.

As I read the account, I felt my heart swell with hope. If men could keep that message of peace on earth and good will towards men, then, surely, they could find ways to avoid conflict. Prayer had been answered. In the kitchen, people looked at one another, amazed yet hardly daring to hope.

At the first chance, I hugged Mother hard. 'Does this mean that it will all come to an end?'

Mother's usually rosy cheeks had grown paler over the past weeks, but now were pink again. 'Ach, mein Liebling, I hope and hope, and pray, but I also fear...'

Her hopes were dashed and her fears not unfounded. The day after this Christmas truce, the guns had started to roar again and there were more dead to be listed.

CHAPTER

The winter dragged by, cold and dreary, week by week. Henry was in France now, and there had been a few letters from him to the manor. They were avidly read and passed from hand to hand by the servants. The first few had been cheery enough.

The training is hard but I'm getting the hang of it, he wrote.

Me and Ben are in the same company, so it's nice to have someone here from home. The lads are a good lot. We have a good few laughs and larks together. We're looking forward to getting over there and knocking the stuffing out of them Jerries.

Polly seemed greatly cheered to hear that the two lads were together.

'I couldn't bear to think of him – them – all alone with strangers. They'll look out for each other.'

Mrs Martin looked at her and shook her head, but said nothing. I guessed she thought Polly was living in a fool's paradise. And maybe she was right, because the next short letters that came were different.

It's tough out here. We had our first stint at the front, and I can tell you it wasn't much fun. I never expected it would be so bad. Back behind the lines now till next time.

Ben's feet are bad and no wonder, we never get to take our boots off. Thank you for the things you sent at Xmas, we were glad of them I can tell you. I think of home a lot when I'm waiting for the next round.

It never seems to stop raining here, the trenches are full of mud and there are rats, they are after the supplies and they're big bold beggars I can tell you...

Polly screamed at this; she was terrified of rats and even mice. Mrs Martin gave her a look and told her to get on with chopping the parsley.

Above stairs, Lady Compton organised 'work parties'. She and her friends met in the sitting room and knitted items to send to the brave soldiers.

'Hugo has a commission,' Harriet told me one dull day in February as we sat in the schoolroom, with Nanny snoring in her chair in the nursery next door. Neither of us went to school, but Harriet was expected to make a show, at least, of 'studying' for part of every day. I no longer felt quite as welcome as before in the upper part of the house, but Harriet had her way as usual.

I looked up quickly from where I had been quietly reading *The Tenant of Wildfell Hall.* I no longer felt a flutter when I encountered, or heard of, the son of the house; the feelings I'd had for him had departed since I'd overheard the conversation with Miss Grey in the rose arbour. But this was big news. 'Has he?'

'Yes. He's joining his regiment in a week. Then he'll be off to France, I expect.' She sighed. 'Lucky him! This place gets duller and duller.'

'Does your mother mind?'

'Oh, Mama has gone all patriotic and boasts to all her friends,' said Harriet. 'She's convinced the war will be won once her darling boy gets over there.'

I was silent. I didn't know what would happen if England won the war. I didn't know what would happen if Germany did. In either case, where would Mother and I fit in? I had no answers.

*

Spring came at last, with the first hint of green in the hedgerows and a chorus of birdsong in the mornings, and then a froth of creamy white on the hawthorns.

Henry wrote wistfully:

A blackbird was singing up on the wire this morning. It made me think of the birds-nesting us boys used to do. I think of home a lot and all of you at the old manor...

There were reports in the papers of a new poison gas being used in the trenches; it burned the lungs. Mrs Martin hid that account from Polly. 'Her having hysterics is all we need,' she said grimly.

One day, a letter arrived addressed to Mother as 'Frau Janina Schmidt' and it had a foreign stamp. I had grown so used to being Emily Smith that the name looked strange and alien. Our village postman had gone to the war, so a woman delivered our post now. She gave Mother a keen look as she handed the letter to her. We seldom received post, and hardly ever from home. Mother's hand shook as she opened the envelope. She had waited for a quiet spell during the busy preparation period before lunch to open it in the bedroom; she beckoned me to come too. As she read, her hand went to her throat and her cheeks paled a little.

'Is it bad news?'

She nodded. '*Ja*. It is from my sister, Gretchen. She says her husband has died, very suddenly, and her son...' she paused and drew a deep breath. 'Her son, Benno, is now serving in the army.'

She sat down on the bed. These were our only relatives, and we had not heard from them for some time. She lifted the letter and continued to read. 'She says – she says, if things are difficult for us here, we may want to return home. It may be best. They would offer us a home with them, and be glad of our help on the farm and in the *Gasthaus*, if guests begin to return.'

She put her hands in her lap, gazing at me strangely, a faraway look in her eyes. I wondered if she wanted to go. She must have guessed my unspoken question, and drew a deep breath. 'I have thought of going back. Especially now. But my lady needs me. She has cared for me, for you. Already some here have left, making more work for the rest. I will stay. I will stay as long as she needs me.'

I let my breath out in a sigh. I did not want to leave either. Bavaria seemed like another world. I wanted to stay, to grow up here, to study, to learn; maybe, one day, to write. The thought came to me in a flash. I wanted to be a writer! How I would achieve it, I did not know, but it was what I wanted.

My mother got up and patted my shoulder. '*Ach*, we will be safe here. The war will end and all will be well.'

But not yet. That very same week, on a fresh May morning, the papers were full of a new disaster. As well as the war news and lists of casualties, a big ocean liner called the *Lusitania*, carrying arms and supplies as well as passengers, had been sunk by German torpedoes off the coast of Ireland, with the loss of more than a thousand souls.

I sensed something different from that day forward. Below stairs, we had jogged along, uneasily sometimes but generally amicably, at least on the surface. Now there was a change: a coldness and hardening. The old gardener dumped the day's vegetables in the scullery, with never a word to Mother, and stamped out. The housemaids looked at us both with newly hostile eyes and refused to talk to us. Even Mrs Martin, normally an example of justice tempered with mercy, said in front of us, 'What a terrible loss of life! Those people are like brute beasts!'

'Dirty Hun!' said Arnold, the sixteen-year-old boy who had taken the place of a footman, with real venom. 'They'll stop at nothing.'

For the first time, I felt afraid. I kept myself to myself and even tried to avoid Harriet. The next day, Mother was summoned upstairs. She went, twisting her apron in her work-worn hands, and returned pale and red-eyed. Without a word, she took my arm and led me to the bedroom. Her hands were shaking and so was her voice.

'We are to leave. They cannot harbour aliens and enemies any longer. They say there has been talk—'

'Talk? What talk?'

'Of spying. Of sending and receiving information.'

I stared. 'Whatever do they mean?'

She pulled out the old suitcase from under the bed, and began to open drawers and pull garments from them, higgledy-piggledy.

'That letter from my sister last week. It is proof they say – a letter from Germany. I must have been sending information and receiving it back.'

'How ridiculous!' I said. 'Didn't you tell Lady Compton that?

Tears welled up in Mother's eyes. 'I did. I offered to show the letter. She believed me. She did not want to let me go, but it is out of her hands. They will give us money, and they told me we must go to my sister. It is the end, Emilie. We cannot stay.'

CHAPTER

Fourteen

We left Compton Manor on a beautiful, early summer morning. A fresh green was on the trees in the park, and sweet white lilac and budding roses were around the arbour. I had not realised just how much I loved the place until I left it. I'd taken it all for granted: the space, the parkland, the beautiful surroundings, the magnificence of the great house that had stood for centuries. Even the cramped little bedroom below stairs Mother and I had shared all those years was suddenly dear to me. It was home.

Mother tried hard to be brave for my sake. Lord and Lady Compton had given us money for our passage home, and more besides. If we could make our way to Bavaria and my aunt Gretchen, we would be safe.

'It is beautiful there,' she told me bravely, tears close to the surface. 'Pine woods and pure, pure air. We will be happy again.'

Saying goodbye was hard for all. Lady Compton wept as we took our leave of her, upstairs in her sewing room. 'I'm sorry, Janina,' she said, embracing my mother. 'It is not my choice, you understand? I would not have done this for the world...'

My mother had to be the one to comfort her. She murmured soothingly to her angel, thanking her and promising always to remember her in her prayers. I stood rather stiffly when Lady Compton embraced me too. I didn't really understand why we were going. How could the war have changed everything, all in the blink of an eye? None the less, it had.

The farewells to the servants were rather more subdued. Some did not even wish us goodbye, pretending to be busy about their tasks. Arnold even smirked. I think they were glad to be rid of us, the enemy in their midst.

Polly whispered in my ear, 'If you should happen to see Henry anywhere, send him our – my – best regards,' as if we were likely to bump into him along the way somehow.

Mrs Martin had a tear in her eye and kissed us both. She said, 'Be safe and be happy, Emilie. Thank you for your years of service, Janina.'

And then we were away, being driven to the station by Beddows, the first and last time we rode in the Silver Ghost.

I had said goodbye to Nanny, who hardly recognised people any more. She said, 'Wrap up warm now, child, there's a chilly wind. And be back in time for tea,' which filled my eyes with tears.

Lord Compton had shaken hands, stiffly. I knew he wished us gone and the stigma of harbouring enemy aliens under his roof removed. His three elder girls had wished us goodbye. Hugo was already away at his army training.

I had dreaded the final parting from Harriet. How I could bid farewell to my lifelong friend and companion I could not imagine. She had raged against our departure the day before, with anger, tears and threats. But on the morning itself, she did not appear and I did not dare ask for her. We could not be late for the train. My heart heavy with grief, I climbed into the back seat of the car with Mother and our modest luggage. We were leaving the sweep of the gravel driveway and heading towards the avenue of beeches when I thought I heard a faint shriek from behind. I turned quickly, and there was a dishevelled little figure bursting from the front porch and running barefoot across the gravel. I almost forgot we were moving and my hand went to the door handle. Mother grasped it and said, 'You can do nothing. Stay still.'

'But it's Harriet!' I said desperately. 'We never said goodbye!'

Beddows must have seen Harriet chasing us in his mirror, but his expression did not change. She ran after the car until her breath gave out. She stopped, throwing up her hands in an attitude of defeat. The car gained speed as it reached the avenue of beeches, their fresh, new green leaves rustling gently. I sat with my head turned to the rear window, tears streaming down my face until we rounded a bend and the forlorn little figure standing on the driveway was lost from view.

*

The fresh summer morning turned into a hot, dusty, confused and exhausting day. We were dropped at the railway station, where Beddows left us without a word of farewell. We heaved our cases inside and queued at the ticket office. For a small, country station, it was very busy, with harassed people hurrying and rushing or anxiously scanning the faces of passengers disembarking from an incoming train. Many were bidding farewell to men in khaki tunics and trousers. Army uniforms and kitbags were everywhere, most of them belonging to fresh-faced boys not much older than I was. They were still enlisting in their scores as soon as they were old enough, or even before, if the tales were to be believed. One of them accidentally jostled me with his kitbag as I waited with the luggage while Mother stood in the queue. I had removed my hat for relief from the warm sticky feeling around its band, and it slipped from my fingers. The young man stooped to pick it up.

'Sorry, darlin'. Clumsy, that's me.'

He had a cheeky, crooked-toothed grin in a round face with skin as pink and smooth as a baby's. Surely he could not be going to war? I thanked him.

He said, 'Pleasure, I'm sure. You seeing someone off? Don't take on. We're going to wipe the floor with the Hun when we get over there and it'll all be over!'

I realised that my woebegone face and tear-stained cheeks were telling their own story. I pulled myself together and started to say, 'No, it's not that, we're—' and then realised with a cold chill that I could not, dare not, tell the truth: that we were 'the Hun', the enemy. The tears started afresh. He said, 'Sorry, darlin'. Didn't mean to upset you. Don't fret too much. We'll all be right as rain. Well, got to go. So long now.'

And he was gone, shouldering his kit and striding cheerfully along the platform to join a group of khaki-clad lads.

My mother was beside me, clutching our tickets. '*Ach*, the trouble I had! Almost they refused me, because of my accent, but then someone else came and it was all right. Who was that you were talking with? Best not to speak to anyone, not to draw attention to ourselves.'

It was a long wait. We sat on a hard bench, with our luggage around us. Mrs Martin had given us a packet of sandwiches as a last gesture of kindness, and we were glad of them. We drank water from the station cloakroom; our money had to be carefully hoarded, so not even a cup of tea could be purchased. I felt more miserable than I could ever have imagined. This was surely the worst day of my life.

Yet more was to come.

CHAPTER

The train came at last to take us on the next part of our journey. We would have to change again, Mother said, before we got the one that would take us to the coast and the possibility of a boat-train to the Continent. It was all uncertain, confusing, frightening and, oh, so tiring. People poured off the train and then others clambered aboard, scrambling for seats. We were lucky; a kind, elderly gentleman offered his seat to us and we squeezed into it together. Mother was so flustered that she forgot herself and said, '*Danke. Dankeschön!*' which caused a few startled looks from those who heard. I felt my cheeks burn, but we were on the train and, before long, there was a whistle, a hiss of steam and we were moving. I looked out of the window through a blur of tears. The scenery flashed past: houses, buildings and then green countryside. All I could feel was an aching void deep inside, born of the knowledge that I was leaving behind all that I knew and loved.

I don't know how long the journey took, but it seemed very long. We finished the last of our sandwiches. We had nothing to drink and I was very thirsty. I noticed one or two curious looks from some of the other passengers. One woman, in particular, stared hard with a look of contempt on her face. I guessed she had heard Mother's unfortunate slip into her native language. Mother gripped my hand hard, whether for her own comfort or mine, I wasn't sure. I whispered to her that if anyone spoke to us, I should be the one to answer. She nodded and bit her lip.

I think I must have dozed on and off through the afternoon, my head on Mother's shoulder. I woke with a start as the train jolted to a stop.

There was a shifting and movement among the passengers. 'We're here,' whispered Mother. We got to our feet, cramped and stiff, and joined the crowd waiting to disembark. The station looked much the same as the one we'd left, bigger perhaps, but again crowded with people, many of them in uniform. And we would have to queue again for the next part of the journey. I saw to our luggage. We got off the train and stood on the platform looking about us.

Suddenly, two men were there, standing, unsmiling, in our way. They wore some kind of uniform too. 'Your names, please?' they asked, addressing Mother.

I was afraid that Mother would reply in German, so I quickly replied, 'We are Janet and Emily Smith.'

The man's eyes flickered over me briefly before resting again on Mother. I saw the fear in her eyes and her lips were trembling. 'Identity papers?' he said curtly.

I guessed we did not have anything with those English names upon them. Had anyone thought we would need papers? I saw Mother's face crumple.

The other man stepped forward and took her arm. 'We have reason to believe you are enemy aliens, from information passed along to us from the last station. You will need to come with us.'

Mother found her voice at last. 'But – but – we are going back to our country. We are leaving.'

The man shook his head. 'I am sorry, madam. You may be a threat to Britain and cannot be allowed to leave. We must investigate. You and your daughter must come with us.'

'But we are not spies!' cried Mother.

The man looked at her coldly. 'I don't believe anyone has mentioned spying,' he said. 'But you must come.'

There was no escape. Mother and I clutched each other and our luggage, and one of the men took her elbow and propelled her firmly through the mass of people.

My heart was thumping hard. My mouth was so dry that I could barely move my tongue. A red mist swam before my eyes and I felt my legs tremble under me.

'Watch out!' said the other man. 'The girl is going to faint!'

I looked up at him and saw through a blur of tears that his expression was not unkind. He took hold of my arm and pushed me down on a seat in the waiting room, shoving aside a couple of other passengers. The faintness passed. I was pulled to my feet, and Mother and I were led to a waiting car. Mother found her voice.

'Where are you taking us? My daughter needs water.'

I saw the first man's lip curl at the sound of her accent. He didn't answer, but the second man found a flask of water and held it to my lips. 'Better now, miss?' he asked. I nodded and thanked him. Mother had a drink too. The first man started the car.

I don't know how long the journey took but, suddenly, the car stopped and we were bundled out and into a building. Unsmiling faces stared at us. Someone demanded our papers and Mother had no choice but to hand them over. We were taken into a bare room and left there, sitting on a hard bench.

'What are they going to do with us?' I asked in a whisper.

She couldn't answer. I had the strange feeling that none of this was real, that, somehow, we were trapped in a nightmare from which we couldn't wake. Time passed.

There were steps outside. Mother and I clutched each other again. A man came in – a different man, in ordinary clothes. He looked closely at us both. 'Well, you are in luck. You will be allowed to travel on and leave the country. In fact, I strongly advise that you do leave as quickly as possible.'

He offered no further explanation. Our papers were handed back to us and we were driven to the nearest railway station with our luggage. The driver even got the tickets and gave them to us, with a small bow and a sort of half-mocking smile. 'Always pays to have good connections,' he said and was gone, leaving us relieved but bewildered.

Mother was deep in thought as we wearily waited for the train. '*Ach*, I have it!' she said, lowering her voice so that no one could hear. 'They saw Lord and Lady Compton's name on the papers. They must have telephoned to them. My angel has come to our rescue once again, may God bless her!'

CHAPTER

Sixteen

We did it. We made the long, wearisome journey by train, boat-train and train again. Days merged into nights; dawn broke in different places. We dozed, woke and dozed again. We left the shores of Britain far behind, travelled many miles overland and finally arrived at my aunt's home in the pine-clad mountains of Bavaria.

The welcome we received was warm, though slightly tempered with a touch of suspicion or maybe reproach; I wasn't sure which. My aunt, a slightly older, thinner version of my mother, was full of questions. Why had we decided to come after all these years? Was it the letter she had written? Hadn't it been taking our lives in our hands to travel with a war raging about us? *Ach*, the war, the cruel, dreadful war! Would we go back when it was all over and the British had been defeated? What was it like to live in an enemy land?

I came to understand that the family had not fully approved of Mother's throwing in her lot with Lord and Lady Compton and moving to a foreign country all those years ago. Nevertheless, my aunt was glad to see us and thankful for the help we would provide. Her husband, Franz, had died of a heart attack very suddenly, and she had been obliged to close the *Gasthaus*. Their son, Benno, had joined the army when war was declared. She, with just the help of a boy from the village, had been left with the work of their small farm: the care of the goats, chickens and geese, the harvest and the woodcutting for the cruel, hard winters. My mother and I would provide two more useful pairs of hands. Maybe the *Gasthaus* could be opened again, when the war was over.

I listened to this conversation, sipping tea and looking about me. Early summer had come to the mountains, and the meadows were ablaze with gentians, primula, clover and many other wildflowers I could not name. Above rose the pine woods that climbed to high peaks hidden in a blue haze. Masses of pink and white fruit blossom clothed the orchards near the house and farm buildings.

The house itself was like something from a fairy tale: long and low, with green painted shutters against white walls, and deep windowsills with railings were already ablaze with red and pink geraniums. Inside were many rooms, but most were shut up now that there were no longer guests. Most of the living went on in the large kitchen, which had solid, wood furniture and a pot-bellied stove. Its windows framed a view of a beautiful valley, with a river and small white houses dotted on its slopes, rising again to the pine-clad mountains.

Aunt Gretchen fed us with a tasty stew, homemade bread and goat's cheese, and put us to bed in a clean, white room, with feather-filled quilts and down pillows – one of the guest rooms.

'Not as grand as your lord and ladyship's great house, I am sure,' she said. 'But there – we all return to our roots when the need arises. You will make do, I'm sure.'

The little hint of sarcasm told me that she had not yet entirely forgiven my mother for her departure.

Mother said hastily, 'Oh, it is so good to be back, and you are so kind, Gretchen.'

My aunt seemed mollified. I couldn't help comparing the spacious, spotless room with the cramped cubbyhole we had shared at Compton Manor.

We slept soundly, worn out from days and nights of travelling, and woke to the sound of birds chirping in the cherry tree outside our window. Mother got out of bed and went to stand at the window.

'It seems so hard to believe that a war is raging,' she said wistfully and sighed. I wondered whether she was sad to have left Compton Manor behind. But she was not thinking of that. 'We were so happy, your father and I. It was a day just such as this that we were married. We felt that our whole lives stretched before us, with endless joys and new discoveries.' She sighed again. 'One day I will take you to see the little house we lived in and where you were born.'

Beautiful as this place was, the English countryside and Compton Manor were home to me. I felt a sharp pang at the thought of them and the memory of Harriet's running, tear-stained, after the car that was taking us away for ever. Harriet was my best friend, the only friend of my age I'd ever known, my forever sister; I had never been apart from her. Now I would never see her again, for I knew we would never go back.

*

We began to grow accustomed to our new life. Mother took on a lot of the work of the house and garden: vegetables were planted and tended; the house was opened up, aired and spring-cleaned from top to bottom. Aunt Gretchen granted that I must keep up my studies, especially as I seemed woefully 'ignorant' of my native language. Although I understood German well, I had always conversed in English. My aunt was also determined for me to learn more of the history and status of our great nation. She was horrified that I had unwittingly referred to Britain as 'our side' when talking about the war. All I'd absorbed in my former life had to be educated out of me. Our land was far superior in culture, art, literature and progress, in any case, and I must leave behind the plebeian ways of the British.

My share of the work was to help the boy, Klaus, in his tasks about the small farm. Klaus came from the village each day. He was a skinny, undersized fourteen-year-old from a large family who needed the money his work brought in. His father and older brother had gone to the war, and Klaus lived for the day when he would be old enough to join them.

'I may go in another year – or two at the most,' he told me with a swagger, as we herded the flock of geese out to their daytime pasture. 'My friend Hans has gone, and he is not all that much older than me.'

I looked at his skinny frame, more suited to a twelve-year-old, and did not see much chance of the army accepting him.

He raised the stick he used for guiding the geese and squinted along it at an imaginary enemy. 'Bang! Bang! That's another two dead British scum! I can't wait!' He swivelled round to point the stick at me. 'Bang! That's another! You're British, aren't you? You ought to be dead too!'

His eyes glittered, and his words sent a cold chill down my spine. I just said coolly, 'I am not British. I was born here. And this war might be over before you're old enough to go.'

'I hope not!' But some of the wind went out of his sails. He lowered his stick and trailed it in the dust. A little boy playing at soldiers, I thought, and felt pity for him. So many of the boys back home had been just the same. And at least two of the lads gone from our village would not return.

I watched the geese scatter over the meadow, tugging at the new, green grass. It was so peaceful, yet, even here, the war spread out its deadly, threatening fingers.

'What is it like, living in an enemy country?' Klaus asked curiously.

I couldn't answer such a question. Even thinking about home brought a huge lump to my throat. I turned and walked back to the house without a word.

CHAPTER
Seventeen

We settled, after a fashion, tucked away in our beautiful, peaceful backwater, while the rest of the world continued in its madness. High summer came: in the meadow, we made fragrant-smelling hay and stored it in the barn for the winter; we picked ripe fruit in the garden and in the woodland; we hoed and weeded the vegetable garden; and picked the first peas of the season. We heard of more countries joining the war. It seemed another world, though my aunt and my mother prayed every day for my cousin Benno and all the others we knew. Mother was careful to keep our prayers for the British lads we knew in the privacy of our bedroom. But we all prayed fervently together for the end of the war.

Autumn came, with busy days of harvesting and woodcutting, the killing of the pig and preparing for the hard winter ahead. The trees were beautiful in their autumn colours. Then winter itself arrived, with a deep cold that I'd never known before, and the mountains were white with snow. We kept our wood stoves well stoked. People and animals hunkered down and waited for the first signs of spring. It came at last, with the first opening of delicate aconites and snowdrops, longer days and increasing warmth. News came of more fighting, including a mighty naval offensive called the Battle of Jutland.

In the summer, there had been another huge conflict called the Battle of the Somme, in which thousands of men on each side had been slaughtered. And, it seemed, Benno was to come home – wounded. Gretchen was frenzied with excitement and apprehension when the news came through. She was torn between joy and relief that her son would return to her and fear of the extent and effect of his wounds. No details had been given in the message.

'What if he has lost a limb?' Gretchen fretted, while polishing the best cutlery to a mirror-like shine.

'I doubt he'll notice a touch of tarnish on his knife and fork,' I thought wryly.

Eating was on my aunt's mind too.

'I have heard that boys are returning without hands or arms,' she continued, 'having to be fed every mouthful, like a tiny child. How Benno would hate that. And I would hate it too, my Benno, my little bear!'

'Let us not worry until we know what we are facing,' said my mother soothingly. 'When we know more, God will give us the courage and strength for each challenge.'

My aunt looked at her sister reproachfully, opened her mouth, no doubt to say that my mother was fortunate to have her child unharmed and safe with her. She closed it again when she remembered how we'd been uprooted and the perilous journey we had taken. My aunt, though worrisome, was a fair and practical person at heart, and knew that we must all pull together in these difficult times.

She managed to smile at me. 'At least he will have the comfort of some young company near his own age when he comes.'

When Benno did arrive, on a sultry day in August, it was with unharmed hands and arms, but with a pale, pinched face and heavy bandaging on his left foot. I remembered nothing of him, and my mother had only memories of him as a small boy at the time she had left the country. The solemn, unsmiling young man in *Feldgrau*, not much older than I was, with close-cropped hair and piercing, blue-grey eyes, was a stranger to me, and I to him.

'So, you are my cousin Emilie,' he said on the morning after his arrival, as I came into the living room. He was sitting with his injured foot on a cushioned stool, his chair placed where he could see the view of the valley from the window. His mother had sent me to ask if there was anything he wanted, while she was off to milk the nanny goats and attend to the dairy work, which she did not entrust to anyone else.

'Yes, I am Emilie,' I said, and explained my errand.

He waved that away impatiently. 'No, no. I am already bloated with food. Half-smothered with kindness and fussing. Unless you can bring about a fast healing.'

I looked at the foot, swathed up to the shin in bandaging. 'Does it pain you a great deal?'

He dismissed that with another impatient movement of his hand. 'The pain doesn't matter. I picked up some cursed infection that makes it slow to heal. I should not be here at all, by rights.' He gazed morosely at the heat haze that was beginning to shimmer across the valley. 'At least it's cooler up here.'

I wondered if my presence irritated him and turned to go. But he spoke again. 'It was shrapnel, you know.'

I hadn't known. The injury had not been discussed in my presence. And then he added, so quietly I could barely hear, 'Thank God.'

That startled me a little.

He glanced at me quickly. 'Better than a bullet wound, though a bullet wound might be cleaner. Gunshot in the foot is suspect. Some cowards do it to themselves, wanting a way out.'

I shuddered. How dreadful that seemed, to be so desperate that to mutilate oneself would seem the only way.

'Would they be sent home, then?' I asked.

He shook his head grimly. 'Court-martialled and then shot for desertion. I've known it happen.' He paused. 'There was a question mark over my injury. My honour was actually in doubt. But the medics soon told them it was genuine. Thank God!'

'Was it so awful at the front then?'

'Bad enough, little cousin. You don't need to know more or you'll be haunted night and day. And you'll fret when I go back.'

I was surprised again. 'You're going back, then?' Somehow, I had imagined that now he had been injured and sent home, the war would be over for him.

A steely look came over his face, bringing a cold glitter to his eyes. 'Of course! We're fighting for the right, for our country, our Fatherland! For all this,' he waved his hand at the peaceful scene framed by the window. 'I can't wait to go back and finish those smug British fools. They're not fit to lick our boots! I'm going to get my foot right and I'm off!'

He had told me that his shattered foot would need time to mend, time for the bones to knit before they would bear his weight. Impatiently, he hopped around on his crutches, wincing with pain whenever the broken bones took weight they were not ready for.

His mother fussed.

'You will always limp if they do not mend right.'

'I don't care about that,' said Benno, the beads of sweat standing out on his forehead. 'Better a limp, and doing my part with my comrades, than sitting useless here.'

'He cannot wait to get back and kill Britons,' said my mother when we were in the privacy of our bedroom. Her voice held sadness and regret. She, like me, remembered those Britons whom we loved and dared not speak highly of now we were back in our own country. I hardly knew how to reply. I didn't want Benno to kill Britons. I thought of Hugo Compton, whom I had fancied myself in love with, and Henry – dear, kind, freckle-faced Henry – and Ben and the village boys from home. I didn't want them dead. With a pang, I remembered John Carter and Joe Walker, already dead and gone. And I didn't want Benno dead either, for I had begun to like him very much.

CHAPTER

Benno's wound was slow to heal, not helped by his impatience and determination to be back at the front lines, which meant he often persisted in pushing himself harder than he should. My aunt's prediction proved true; as the bones slowly knit together and Benno walked again, it was with a limp. He shrugged this off as unimportant.

In the weeks of autumn, while harvests were gathered in, I accompanied him on his walks, which he insisted on lengthening day by day. I could see the pain it caused him, and the relief when I suggested it was time to sit and rest for a while.

During these rest times, sitting on a tree stump or a low wall, Benno would often ask about my life, how it had been living in the enemy country before Mother and I returned.

'Did it not make your skin crawl, being a servant in that outlandish place?' he asked curiously one day, when yellow leaves were beginning to fall from the fruit trees.

I barely knew how to answer. It was hard, having been the suspect foreigner back in a place I considered home and also being regarded with suspicion now that we were back in our own land. My lips twisted. To hear the gracious way of life at Compton Manor described as outlandish seemed ironic. After all, here I regularly cleaned out goat, pig and poultry pens, and piled the manure in a heap for fertilizing the vegetable garden. I was often confused, but I felt I must be honest above all else.

'I was not a servant,' I said. 'Mother was the cook at Compton Manor, but nothing was required of me. I shared a schoolroom with the daughter of the house.'

It may have sounded grander than it was, even a little boastful, although I did not mean to be.

Benno gave me a strange look. 'All the same, you must be glad to be back among your own.'

I didn't answer that. Talking of the schoolroom had brought back memories of Harriet, the way we had spent almost all our waking hours together and had shared everything, and how the war had cruelly torn us apart. Tears filled my eyes.

Benno was still looking at me; I sensed his attitude harden a little. 'Surely you cannot be homesick for those people and that place.'

I was and would say so if he pressed me. But then he seemed to soften again and said, 'It is hard to have change thrust upon one. But it is beautiful here too, is it not?'

I looked down the valley, where the trees were in autumn shades of orange and russet, brown and yellow, and had to agree with him. I had come to love the view of the hills, forests and meadows, where all kinds of wildflowers bloomed and bees buzzed about them. I loved the flowers themselves, some of them familiar to me and some not. There was one among them, a small, blue, bell-shaped bloom that hung on a curved stem. It had blossomed since early spring and was still flowering now, later in the year. There was one near my feet; I picked it and held it up for Benno to see.

'It is beautiful and I love the wildflowers, especially this one. Do you know what it is called?'

He took it and held it gently. 'It is called a fairy thimble. See how the petals make the shape of a little thimble? I used to put them on my fingers when I was small. Then, later on, I wrote a poem about them.'

I was surprised. 'You wrote a poem?'

Benno reached over and stuck the little flower in the buttonhole of my pinafore. 'There! It matches the blue of your eyes. Yes, I wrote lots of poems. I still do, in fact. Only now they're not so carefree.'

My cousin was proving to be a person of many sides. I felt a sudden warmth towards him and said, with a burst of confidence, 'I want to be a writer! I don't know what kind or what I will write about, but it's what I want to do.'

He looked at me for a moment, then said, 'Maybe you could start by writing me some letters when I go back. We all look forward to letters from home. Mother writes, but she is not much of a scribe. She mostly sends instructions to keep my feet dry and be sure to get enough sleep.' He laughed a little ruefully. 'If she knew.'

'Oh, I will—' I began to say but we were interrupted by the appearance of Klaus, who hung around Benno whenever he could and loved to hear details of a soldier's life at the front. Benno never told him much, at least, not when I was present. But when Klaus was around, I noticed my cousin always grew a little more boastful, a hint of swagger and bravado in his attitude. I did not much like him in that mood, especially when they began to express their contempt for the British. I got up.

'I'm going back to the house now,' I said. 'If you need assistance, I'm sure Klaus will help you.'

I thought I heard a snigger as I went, although I might have been mistaken, and felt hurt. Klaus never missed a chance to take a dig at my British connections. I'd been feeling that Benno and I might have a real friendship, but that feeling was now shattered. He was a man and a soldier first and foremost. Maybe he was already regretting sharing his inner thoughts with me. A sob rose in my throat, so I quickened my footsteps in case they heard and laughed at me.

CHAPTER
Nineteen

Suddenly, it seemed, winter was upon us again: the harvests gathered in, the trees bare, the pig killed and salted away for winter use, and the first frosts whitening the grass. And before Christmas came, Benno was gone, still limping but with a glint of resolve in his eyes, to join his unit.

'They could at least have let him spend Christmas at home,' mourned Aunt Gretchen. 'I miss him so much, my Benno, my little bear.' But she comforted herself with the thought that he had already been injured, had already received his war wound, which surely meant he would be safe from now until the war ended. Mother and I were doubtful about the logic of that, but we kept our thoughts to ourselves, not wanting to dampen my aunt's optimism. She was enthusiastic when I told her Benno had asked me to write to him and encouraged me to do so. I was nothing loath. I had begun to keep a journal, telling of the war and how my life had changed. It helped, somehow, to clear my mind and make sense of a world and circumstances turned upside down. I would have dearly loved to write to Harriet, but letters between two warring nations would be unwise if not impossible. I sometimes had the fanciful idea that, some day, Harriet would read what I had written, and the years between would melt away. Writing to Benno might not mean so much to me, but I was willing to do so. He had told me how much the boys welcomed news from home.

So our correspondence began, brightening the long, dreary winter and bringing some interest to the tedium of our days.

In early January, I wrote:

There is snow on the hills now and, when the sun shines, it glistens like the icing on one of my mother's strudels. Here, we have flurries that blot out the valley but, so far, no covering that has lasted. There's a piercing wind that brings tears to the eyes and seems to cut right through to the bone. Even the goats don't like to be outdoors, but huddle around the doorway when they are let out, waiting to be let back in again. Their milk sometimes begins to freeze in the pail before we can get back to the dairy. We had a nice Christmas, but you were very much missed. We put up the Christmas tree and sang carols around it on Christmas Eve. Before then, we had the business of killing the geese, plucking them and preparing them for the Christmas market. Ugh! I did not like that at all, and I shed a tear for those creatures I had taken care of all summer and autumn. But I'm glad to say I forgot my sadness when roast goose was served up for Christmas dinner!

And how are you, Cousin Benno? We pray it is not as cold there as it is here in the mountains. Did you receive the parcel we sent? We are now busy knitting more scarves, socks and gloves in the long, dark evenings. We hope they will be a comfort. The other day I had the notion that the countries might cease the fighting in winter and then begin again in spring, if they had to. But then I realised how foolish that sounded, like people playing a game of chess or farmers planning their crop growing.

I will close now as I have my jobs to do. You are always in our prayers.

Your loving cousin,

Emilie

Aunt Gretchen wrote to her son too, but her letters were short and practical as he had predicted, giving instructions for his welfare and remedies for everything from chilblains to constipation. She could not understand what on earth I found to write long letters about, but I sensed that she was glad I did.

We waited a long time for replies from Benno. There were delays and difficulties with communications, not helped by winter weather. Here in the mountains, the real snow, when it came, sometimes cut us right off for days. When I did get a letter, snowdrops were out nodding their white heads and bringing a promise of spring.

I often think of you, little cousin, and of home, **Benno wrote.**

When I read your letter, I can picture it all, just as you describe. I remember those winters so well, the sledging and skating when the village pond froze over. Here, it is cold. No snow but mud, mud, mud. Even when we're not in the trenches and back behind the lines for a spell, it is unbelievably dreary. I was glad to get letters from home. Don't tell Mother, but I haven't yet used the chilblain remedy she sent. I don't even know if I have them. Our feet are always painful and sometimes we don't even take our boots off for days. My injured foot pains me a little.

I guessed this meant it hurt quite a lot. He went on:

Christmas was quiet here, but we celebrated in our own way. No offensives, so we opened our parcels from home and enjoyed the contents. Especially the tobacco, sweets and other things to eat. Someone had some bottles of beer, so we had quite a merry time of it and sang a few songs – some of them not ones I would like you or Mother to hear!

It's good to hear of the snowdrops pushing up. Such a brave little flower in the middle of last year's detritus. After them will come the aconites, crocuses, daffodils and all the spring flowers. Then not long until those little fairy thimbles that you like so much! I wish I could see them all.

There is talk of a big offensive to come when the weather is right. Pray for me, little cousin.

The letter ended:

I must now write to my mother. Please write again. Your words bring home to life like nothing else. Sometimes, here, it is hard to imagine another life, but your letters make it all real and bring hope. You have a gift. However this war ends, whatever the future holds, you must use that gift for words.

Part Three
Harriet

Twenty

I felt I could never forgive them for what they did to me on the day that Emilie and Janina left us for ever.

'The dressmaker will be coming this morning to do a fitting for your new dresses,' my mother told me at breakfast on that fateful day. 'You have grown so much in this past year that nothing you have will do for another summer.'

I knew that I had grown, although not as much as Emilie, who was taller than her mother now, and far more slender and graceful than I. In long skirts, with her hair up, she would pass for seventeen or eighteen. I would always be on the dumpy side, though I was now a little taller; my skirts no longer reached to mid-calf and my bodices had become tight.

'She will bring fabric patterns and you may choose the ones you like,' said Mama. I had never been allowed to choose before. For a moment, I was distracted, then the lump of misery in my stomach reminded me that this was the day of parting.

'I don't want to be fitted,' I said. 'Can't she come another day? Emilie is leaving this morning. I am going to stay with her every single moment.'

My mother sighed and looked at my father. I knew what the look meant: 'We might have known she'd be awkward and make a scene'. Then her lips pursed. 'No, I cannot change the arrangements. There will be time enough to say your goodbyes.'

So for hours, it seemed, I stood in my petticoat while the dressmaker measured and scribbled and measured again, and draped material around me with her mouth full of pins.

Maybe I judged my parents too harshly; maybe they genuinely got the time wrong. But I firmly believe that they had planned the whole thing to keep me out of the way, when the car came for Janina and Emilie, in case I should upset everyone unnecessarily by making a scene. I was standing on a stool, for the dressmaker to measure and mark the hemline, when I heard a car engine turn over at the garage, which the schoolroom overlooked. It spluttered and roared into life, then I heard the crunch of gravel under tyres, and it stopped again. Doors opened and shut, and there was the sound of voices.

And then I knew.

I jumped down from the stool, almost knocking over the kneeling dressmaker, who gave a startled little cry and spat out some pins. I ran from the room in my petticoat, down the stairs and out through the kitchen entrance, Swiss dotted muslin fabric floating around me, pins scattering in all directions. The little group of servants gathered there turned to look at me and one or two mouths fell open.

But I was too late. The car was already pulling away down the drive. 'Stop! Stop! Stop!' I screamed, running after it as fast as I could, forgetting that my feet were bare and not feeling the sharp gravel under them, forgetting everything except that Emilie was leaving and I had not even said goodbye. I caught a glimpse of her face, white and startled, looking out from the back window of the motor. Then the car had gathered speed and disappeared round the bend, into the avenue. They were gone.

I stood there, sobbing, until Mrs Martin came and put her arm round my shoulders. She said, 'Come inside, my lamb. Look, your feet are bleeding. Don't take on so.' She glanced sideways at Hannah and said, 'This is what happens!'

I didn't know what she meant and cared not at all. My mother must have come down because I remember her expression, one of shock and concern, and that she put a cloak round me and led me inside. I broke away and ran up the stairs, bursting into the old nursery where Nanny sat.

I flung myself down beside her and buried my face in her lap, my whole body racked with sobs. And Nanny, poor dear Nanny, not understanding what was going on, stroked my head and said, as she had so many times, 'There, there, my pet. It will all be better soon.'

I could not forgive them for deceiving me in such a cruel way. Mama tried to explain. 'We thought this was the best way. It would have made it so much harder for you. For you both – Emilie as well.'

'Emilie was my friend!' I burst out. 'My only friend! I just wanted to say goodbye! We were forever sisters, and we never even said goodbye!' And then I was sobbing again.

Mama didn't remark on my reference to 'forever sisters', probably putting it down to my overdramatic nature and the fact that I was at an 'awkward' age, as I'd heard her say to a friend at one of her knitting work parties. She tried to be kind and understanding but, after a while, her patience wore thin. Times were hard enough without an adolescent daughter having tantrums over something that couldn't be helped. My father completely dismissed all the fuss as female histrionics and became exasperated with me. Margaret tried to be kind, but she was preoccupied with some business of her own. The servants were awkward around me. Lacking a cook, and several other staff members, they were run off their feet, for they had to attend to our needs no matter what went on in the wider world.

I sulked and fumed, refused to study and wouldn't eat at mealtimes. Although, when the coast was clear, I would sneak down to the kitchen and help myself. And every night, despite being proud of the fact I seldom cried, I sobbed myself to sleep.

How long this would have gone on for, I don't know, but my bout of self-pitying misery was brought to an end by three important events, which shook us all to the core and meant that our lives would never be the same again.

First, Nanny died suddenly, sitting upright in her rocking chair, as she had sat for so long, watching over the nursery and her charges. She had always been there, a constant figure in my life; one that I completely took for granted but unconsciously counted on long after I had left the nursery.

We laid her to rest in the little village churchyard and all of us wept, even, I was sure, my father. But there was an undertone of relief too: Nanny had become increasingly forgetful and had needed continual care. I could not believe she was gone and missed her unbearably, the foundation of my world shaken afresh.

The second bombshell was dropped by Margaret: she had decided to join the VADs or, to give the full title, the Voluntary Aid Detachment, which had been set up to provide civilians to assist qualified nurses in caring for wounded soldiers.

Mama was aghast. 'But you could be sent to France! Even to the field hospitals near the front lines! Your life could be in danger!'

Margaret shrugged. 'At least I'd be of some use. Not just sitting, twiddling my thumbs.'

Nothing Mama could say would change her mind. She had already applied and been accepted, she said, and would be off to London to begin her training in a few weeks.

But even Margaret's decision paled into insignificance when the third bombshell fell. Papa gathered us together on a Sunday morning after church and broke the news. He didn't beat about the bush. Compton Manor was to be requisitioned as a hospital for convalescent officers. We would shortly be leaving here and moving into the lodge.

CHAPTER

Twenty-One

Papa's news couldn't have shocked us more than if a real bomb had dropped on Compton Manor.

'A hospital – here?' cried my mother. 'With sick people?'

'That is usually the function of a hospital,' said my father dryly. 'Though, in this case, it will be wounded and convalescent soldiers. Officers injured and maimed in the service of their country. Our country,' he said. Seeing that there were questions on several pairs of lips, he held up his hand and added, 'I was asked and I could not refuse. It will not be permanent. It is the least we can do.'

I knew my father was quietly frustrated that he was no longer eligible for active service himself, and that my mother was glad of it. But this had thrown her into a real state of consternation. She sank back in her chair and clutched her throat.

'But – the house! Our house – full of sick men! And there will be doctors and nurses… how can we live like that?'

'I have told you, Sophia,' said my father, who clearly had given no thought to my mother's feelings before today, 'we will be moving to the lodge for the duration. Bennet and his wife will move to their daughter's cottage in the village and we will move in. The hardships will do us no harm.'

My mind was whirling with myriad questions.

Margaret said eagerly, 'Maybe I could help with the nursing until I start my own training?' Louisa said, 'Yes, we could do that.' I had an inkling that Louisa's motives were more to do with the possibility of meeting dashing, young officers than caring for the sick.

'You could not,' said my father. 'Some of those brave fellows are seriously maimed and have grievous wounds of the sort I could not even describe to you. It will be no place for young ladies. There will be nurses who are properly trained and qualified.'

Caroline looked perplexed. 'But where will they all go, all the beds and the hospital equipment?'

'The ballroom and large dining room will be the main wards – other rooms designated for treatments, consultations and so on. We must get ready, clear the rooms and prepare the house, and ourselves, for changes.'

My mother had appeared to be on the edge of a swoon, but I knew she was stronger than she seemed. Accepting the inevitable, she pulled herself together and began to make plans. The rooms must be cleared, the good things stored, furniture protected, and paintings, ornaments and valuables removed to safety. The servants must be instructed – goodness gracious! What of the servants? Were they to come to the lodge each day?

My father was growing a little impatient. Most of the servants would be required to stay to perform the domestic duties required at the manor. We would not need them all at the lodge; only a cook and, perhaps, a housemaid or parlourmaid. We girls must set to and take on some of the work ourselves. He fixed us with an eagle eye that brooked no argument.

*

And so it was. In a surprisingly short space of time, the house was transformed: carpets were rolled, furniture shifted and valuables stored; and rows of hospital beds, lockers and all the paraphernalia of a hospital were installed. The resident nursing staff would sleep in our bedrooms, minus the more luxurious items and the things we took with us. The servants would prepare the food and do the cleaning and other tasks.

Very soon afterwards, a fleet of ambulances drew up, one by one, on the gravelled forecourt and disgorged their loads: men on stretchers, men on crutches, men missing limbs and men swathed in bandages. It was useless for Papa to forbid us to watch; we couldn't help it. We were drawn to the compelling sight of so many wounded men. After a few days, when they had settled in, some of the men emerged again into the fresh air, in bath chairs or on crutches, to sit on the terrace or the lawn. If they were able, they took gentle exercise walking in the grounds, always with a nurse or even two in attendance.

We settled into the lodge, after a fashion. It seemed dreadfully small and cramped, and there were only three bedrooms and a small boxroom. Mama and Papa had the biggest room; Louisa and Caroline shared one, and Margaret and I had the third. Mama bore the change with admirable fortitude, with scarcely more than a heavy sigh from time to time. Louisa grumbled. Caroline spent as much time as she could out of doors, with the horses and the dogs. I felt confined and frustrated. Margaret left the lodge a great deal to go to our old home; she said she was mostly in the kitchen, learning to cook from Hannah, who had been promoted from head housemaid and was now the Compton Manor cook. I suspected Margaret spent as much time, or more, flitting about the house, hobnobbing with the nurses or even the patients.

Once we had left the big house, I felt a strange reluctance to go back there. It took me a while to realise why, and I understood only when I had been to the kitchen one day, with Margaret, to bring back some vegetables for our use at the lodge. The kitchen was as busy as ever, or even busier, with so many invalids and their carers to cater for. Some of the men required special diets, and there was a shortage of staff. I stood and watched them fly about, fetching, carrying, mixing and chopping – none taking any notice of me at all. Even Mrs Martin was closeted in her room with seemingly endless lists of meals, needs and requirements. But it wasn't that. It was the absence of Emilie that I felt so keenly. She had always been there and now she wasn't. Without her, in spite of all the bustle, the kitchen seemed a lonely place.

I returned to the lodge that day feeling as though I didn't care if I never went back to my old home again. I didn't like the smell of carbolic soap, disinfectant and other, less pleasant, odours that hung about. I resented the doctors and nurses who tramped up and down our grand staircase, now stripped bare of its green carpet, as though it belonged to them. I didn't much care for the glimpses of the walking wounded that I saw about the grounds; they were stooped or hobbling and shuffling like old men, although they had so recently been proud, young officers.

I did not go to the house again for a long time. The war went on, without any prospect of its ending. The future looked bleak.

CHAPTER
Twenty-Two

The seasons were changing again; summer drifted into autumn. Margaret departed for London and her VAD training, and then to her first posting in a London hospital. She wrote occasionally:

It's hard work, we're oh so busy, and every day we must walk miles, up and down corridors and flights of stairs, back and forth to our lodgings. Sometimes I seem to do little else but scrub floors and deal with bedpans. But the lads are so grateful for everything we do, it makes it all worthwhile, despite the dragon of a sister we have.

'She sounds happy,' I thought wistfully, and chewed my pen trying to think of something interesting I could tell her.

Then, one day, we had a visit from Mrs Martin, carrying a basket containing a shepherd's pie for our supper. She looked a little flustered. My mother told me to invite her in and ask if she'd like a cup of tea. Mrs Martin declined the tea, but sat on the edge of a dining-room chair and said she had something to ask.

'It's like this, my lady. Things are difficult up at the manor. What with all those men, never mind the nurses and doctors, we are hard put to it to manage. It's mostly the cooking and such. Hannah does her best, but she's no match for Janina, and the rest of us are run off our feet.' She paused. Mama frowned a little.

'What do you want us to do, Mrs Martin? We tried to hire more staff, if you remember, but there's none to be found. We can fend for ourselves a little more here, if that would help? I am learning to cook a little.'

I hid a wry smile. Mama had made a few half-hearted attempts, it was true, which had resulted in burned fingers, scorched pans and food that was barely edible. Louisa had recently begun a correspondence with a young army major on active service, on which basis she was already beginning to sew a trousseau. Caroline was never indoors. I felt two pairs of eyes turn to look at me.

'I just wondered, your ladyship,' said Mrs Martin hesitantly, 'whether Lady Harriet would come and give us some assistance at the manor? We could give her some cookery lessons. Another pair of hands would make all the difference.'

I knew exactly what Mama's reaction would be and how she would answer. 'Oh, but Harriet is still studying, and we wish her to continue. We would not like her to be exposed to distressing scenes of the kind there must be at the manor. Besides, I do not think that such work would appeal to her.'

They both looked at me. The prospect did not appeal much, but I felt a perverse spirit rise up in me. I said, 'Oh, but it would! I should love to learn how to cook!'

Mrs Martin said quickly 'I would supervise carefully, and she would not have any contact with the hospital side, my lady.'

Mother did not argue further. The next day, I began my work in the manor kitchen. It was more mundane than I'd expected, but I did learn some basics of cookery: to make pie pastry and weigh out ingredients; to roast and baste, and broil and marinade. I balked at learning to pluck and dress poultry and game; the very sights and smells turned my stomach. So Mrs Martin and Hannah spared me that, leaving me instead to peel, scrape, chop and dice mounds of potatoes and other vegetables. There were special diets for those requiring them, and the fitter, recovering men ate huge amounts, or so it seemed, and made stacks of washing up.

I was scraping carrots at the sink one morning when, glancing up and out of the window, I noticed a young man sitting in a bath chair on the grass, under the chestnut tree, apparently staring into space. I had seen him there before, always motionless, and I was curious.

'Is he badly injured?' I asked.

Hannah shook her head. 'I don't know. He spends hours just sitting. I think they call it shell shock.'

'He looks lonely,' I said, and plopped a carrot into a saucepan.

Hannah looked at me. I think she sometimes found me more of a trial than a help.

'Well, when you've stopped day-dreaming and finished those carrots, you can take this cup of beef tea out to him. He has one about now'.

The young man did not look up as I approached. His gaze was on the flowering shrubs, but it was as though he were not seeing them.

I put the cup down on the little table beside him and said, rather foolishly, 'I brought your beef tea.'

He did look up then and I was shocked. He was much younger than I'd thought: no more than two or three years older than I was, and yet so old – haggard, sunken-cheeked and grey-skinned. His hair was light brown, with a hint of curl; his eyes hazel, sunken, dead-looking and, oh, so weary. A few healed scars showed on his face. He did not thank me or answer in any way. He did not pick up the cup and, after a moment, dropped his head again.

I did not know what to do. Hannah was at the kitchen window and I had to go back. On the way, I met one of the nurses I'd seen about.

She said, 'Oh, you've taken Edward his drink, Lady Harriet. Thank you.'

I could not get the young man's face out of my mind. I blurted out, 'He looks so tired!'

She stopped, lowering her voice. 'He doesn't sleep. He twitches and jerks and tosses about, and if we give him a sleeping draught, he wakes screaming with terrible nightmares—'

'Was he badly wounded?'

'He had some shrapnel wounds; they're healing. It's not that. It's his mind. Shell shock. All the men in his command were wiped out. He never speaks. He only ever says two words: "My men! My men!". Never eats – I shall have to coax him to drink that beef tea.' She stopped, perhaps realising that she was saying too much. Hannah tapped on the window. We hurried on our separate ways.

I could not get the young man out of my mind. I learned he was Captain Edward Miller. He had been wounded in battle and had been the only survivor of his command. Day after day, he sat under the chestnut tree, grey-faced and staring into space.

It was the ward sister who had the idea of me sitting with him, maybe reading aloud. She thought that perhaps someone near his age, that a young voice, would help to bring his mind back from wherever it had gone. I did not dare tell Mama and swore Mrs Martin to secrecy. But, the next day, I took along a book of poems from the schoolroom. After lunch, I began to read to him from Tennyson's poem 'The Brook', while sitting on a little stool I'd set down beside his bath chair:

'I come from haunts of coot and hern,

I make a sudden sally and sparkle out among the fern, to bicker down a valley.'

I read, letting the soothing cadence and familiar words wash over us both. I went on to Wordsworth's 'Daffodils', hoping it would revive pleasant memories to replace the dreadful ones. He did not show any interest, but I noticed that when I paused, his head would lift for a moment and his eyes would focus on me. On and on I read, thankful beyond measure that Miss Grey had taught me to read slowly, and to pronounce clearly the words and syllables. I was still reading when the nurse, whom I'd met the day I first noticed Edward, brought out the beef tea.

'Oh!' she said.

I feared I had stayed too long and started to apologise.

'No,' she said. 'Look!' I looked at Edward and saw that his head had fallen back against the headrest. His eyes were closed and he was fast asleep. Some of the greyness seemed to have faded; he looked peaceful and young again.

'Oh!' said the nurse again. 'It's the first natural sleep he's had since he got here. It will do him a great deal of good. Thank you so much."

She tucked the blanket around him and began to wheel the chair away. Edward did not stir. 'Sleeping like a baby,' said the nurse. 'Thank you, Lady Harriet.'

I felt a warm glow. For perhaps the first time in my life, I had made a difference.

CHAPTER
Twenty-Three

I sat with Edward several other times that autumn, reading and sometimes just talking to him, though I was not a good conversationalist, especially when the other person did not respond. But the nurses told me that he had changed dramatically, and I noticed some change myself. The greyness had gone from his skin and the deadness from his eyes. He was eating a little better and his face was filling out, the terrible gauntness fading. He still stared into space and did not speak, but I was told that he slept better and that the nightmares had lessened. And then, one day, as I was closing my book and preparing to leave, he said two words, and they were not the two anguished words that he had repeated over and over. He simply said, 'Thank you.'

I went home elated and could not resist telling Mama of my success in helping a sick man. She was surprised and not very pleased, but did not forbid me to continue. I think she may even have been a little proud of me, although, of course, she would not say so. Heaven forbid that I should grow conceited!

However, my visits with Edward came to an abrupt end. I caught a cold, which kept me indoors for a week. Then it began to rain: a dreary, grey autumn rain that turned the fallen leaves to slippery slush and prevented the convalescents from spending time outdoors. I went back to the manor kitchen and did my tasks there, but that was all.

Time passed. The convalescent soldiers came and went, some to their homes, some back to their regiments to continue their part in the conflict. One or two, sadly, left this life for the next. There had been a suicide, which the kitchen staff talked about in hushed voices. The poor fellow had been unable to face another day of life. For an instant, I had a terrible fear that it was Edward, but then I remembered that he had departed for home. Even so, something rose inside me and I could not be silent, even to my mother. Filled with rage, I declared, 'If someone had been there to talk to that man and listen to him, this might not have happened!'

She put down the knitting she was working on. 'That man was shell-shocked. He could not be helped. You must not dwell on these things.'

I was indignant and stamped my foot in exasperation. I was well past my sixteenth birthday but still behaved like a child sometimes. Maybe that was why my parents still treated me as one.

'He could have been helped! Even *I* could have helped him – if I'd had the chance!'

Mama sighed and laid aside her knitting. 'I'm really wondering if it's good for you to be at the manor so much, listening to the kitchen gossip. I'm beginning to think it's not healthy, with all those sick men close by. You are too young for such things. Your mind is still being formed—'

I flounced off. It was no use arguing. I went upstairs to my room – my own room, now that Margaret was gone. I think my parents were at a loss to know what to do with me. My three sisters had all gone to a school in Switzerland at my age to be 'finished' – that is, to learn to be young ladies. Louisa had taken to it like a duck to water; Caroline and Margaret had both hated it. The war, of course, had put paid to any plans for my own 'finishing'. My mother opined that we should be looking forward and planning for my 'coming out' season in London. Otherwise, how would I ever find a husband? Fortunately, Louisa seemed to have found someone and would be well on the way to matrimony once her officer returned. Caroline and Margaret, on the other hand, were 'out' too but neither had any attachment. Were they doomed to be old maids? This war was so terrible.

I did not think Caroline and Margaret were unhappy at all, old maids or not. Caroline still spent much of her time with the horses and, with the two younger grooms gone to the army, old Hobbs was glad of her help. She had also taken it on herself to manage part of the day-to-day running of the Home Farm and, because so many men had gone, she often carried out the practical tasks that had to be done. My mother tut-tutted a little; my father was glad to have some of the responsibility lifted from his shoulders. Caroline worked long hours and often came in, exhausted and smelling of sweat and manure, to wash, eat and retire early to bed in preparation for another hard day. But I knew she was happy.

Margaret had finished her training and was well into her first placement in a busy London hospital. I missed her most of all. We had never been particularly close, but her going left a big gap in my life. I wrote to her and she replied, rather to my surprise. She said that she was very busy but, reading between the lines, I sensed that she missed home as well. *'I will be on duty over Christmas, so will not be able to come home,'* she wrote.

It will be strange for you, won't it, being at the lodge for Christmas. Do you remember the ten-foot-high Christmas tree we had in the hall? You'll have to get a tiny one this year. And I wonder what will happen about the staff parties and the Christmas boxes?

Christmas was indeed a muted affair, quiet and quite miserable, I thought. I helped to stir Christmas puddings and make mince pies for the patients. We were all invited to a party at the manor on Christmas Eve. We sang carols and drank mulled wine, and everyone tried to make it as happy a time as they could for the wounded men. For me, at least, it was not very merry but, then, as Mother once remarked to me, perhaps it was just that I was determined to be miserable. I still missed Emilie dreadfully.

In the New Year came another letter from Margaret:

Guess what? I am being transferred to another hospital, possibly Southampton or one of the ports where we will be treating men returning fresh from the battlefields! It is rather daunting but I am looking forward to it. Before then, I have a few days leave. It is hardly worth the bother of coming home, but I was wondering, Harry, if Mother and Father would let you come and visit? I'd love to see you, and I could show you a bit of London. What do you think? Please say you'll come, Harry!

The very thought made my heart leap! To get away from this boredom, this dull routine, this dreary winter landscape, if only for a few days. Margaret said I could get the train and she would meet me at Paddington Station. She would write to Mama and Papa. There was plenty of room for us both in Papa's town apartment.

As expected, my parents were not keen on the idea, especially my travelling alone. My father seldom went to the capital these days, being burdened with his responsibilities for the estate, and because of the pain from his gout, which was always worse in the winter damp. My mother fretted about the journey but was eventually persuaded that not much could happen to me between being put on the train at our end and being met by Margaret at the other. I had a ream of instructions about what to do and what not to do, and advice I must remember. I would travel first class to be away from people. Mama did not say 'common people' but that is what she meant. I must not speak to strangers. I must not fall asleep. I must do this and not do that – the instructions came until my head rang. My bag was packed with far too many clothes for a few days.

On the day, my mother showed that she was putting on a brave face. I could not help a wry smile; anyone would think she was seeing me off to the front lines instead of a pleasant visit with my sister. My father was more practical: he pressed some banknotes into my hand, more than I would need. I kissed them both and climbed into my first-class carriage. I took one last look at them. They seemed small and lonely somehow, standing together on the platform. Then there was a great hiss of steam, the whistle blew and we were off.

CHAPTER
Twenty-Four

The journey was uneventful and my carriage was not overcrowded, although there was a great crush and bustle of bodies, many in uniform, on the rest of the train and on the platform. Margaret met me at Paddington and we got a taxi-cab to our father's rooms. London was grey and its streets wet, but it was another world and I was entranced. So many people and traffic; so much movement. Such a change from brown, muddy, winter fields and the slower pace of life in Herefordshire. Here, everyone moved with purpose and haste, all with their part to play in the drama of a country at war. It was raining, buildings were stark and colourless, faces were set and serious, and I was thrilled as I had never been before.

I settled quickly into our comfortable quarters. Margaret was so pleased that I was there. The cooking skills I'd learned at home in the manor kitchen would come in useful, she said with a grin, as her own domestic efforts were mediocre to say the least. She was expecting details of her posting at any moment, she told me, and was looking forward to the new challenges.

In the meantime, she would show me some of the sights of London. We walked down the Mall to Buckingham Palace. We saw the Tower of London, with its ravens, and we walked by the muddy waters of the Thames and watched various craft negotiating Tower Bridge. When our feet began to ache, we had tea at a Lyons Corner House, which I thought to be very modern and sophisticated.

I learned that, here in London, we must do other domestic chores as well as cooking; Margaret said we had to put our privileged upbringing behind us and live as others did. I thought wryly that this was a bit contradictory, as we were enjoying the comfort of a spacious flat, rent-free, and even had someone who came in daily to do the heavy cleaning.

In the evenings, we sat on the hearthrug in front of the fire, drank cocoa and talked. Margaret and I had never been particularly close; I had always been very much the baby sister, but now the years between us seemed to fall away. I think she was glad to have me there and, in spite of her fascinating new life, glad to have a little part of home for a while. I even felt able to tell her a little about the heartbreaking gap that Emilie had left in my life. When I told her how Emilie and I had called her friends the Suffering Jets, she laughed.

'Have you given that all up, now that you're a nurse?' I asked.

She shook her head. 'I wouldn't say I'm exactly a nurse, not in the eyes of qualified nurses, anyway,' she said. 'They tend to look down their noses at VADs. But, yes, I still believe in women's rights. And I think this war will change everything. Women are already doing the work of men. When it's all over, I think things will have changed for ever.'

She spoke passionately, and I was impressed. I felt something else too – almost an envy – that she had a place and a purpose, that her life would count and she would make a difference.

The time passed quickly – too quickly. The night before I was to return, I said, gazing at the glowing fire, 'I wish I could stay longer. I don't want to go home.'

She looked at me for a moment without replying. I'd noticed that her cheeks had lost their teenage chubbiness and that she had changed into someone more serious than the laughing, carefree girl she had been.

'Then don't, Harry. This place is always here, even if I'm not. You've learnt your way around and to take care of yourself. Why not stay a while longer?'

I stared at her. 'But they'd never let me stay longer! It was hard enough getting them to let me come for a few days, with you here!'

She nodded, tucking her long skirt under her knees, and said thoughtfully, 'Mother and Father will probably kill me for encouraging you, but I think you're right. You're wasting your life away at home. They never quite approved of me coming to London, but I think they're impressed with how I've stuck to it.'

I sat for a while, holding my cup of cocoa and watching the flames. It was cosy here with the curtains drawn, but I could still hear the faint hum of a city going about its business. I felt a flicker of excitement rise within me.

I thought of going back to Compton Manor and tamely helping with Mother's war efforts: knitting mounds of socks, scarves and mittens, and organising parcels of 'comforts'. I felt rebellion grow. I was young; I was strong; I hated the war, but it was happening. Surely I could make a difference.

'I'm going to telephone Mother and Father,' I said. 'Tell them I want to stay in London. I'm not a baby. They can't make me go home.' Margaret nodded again. 'I could introduce you to some people at the Red Cross, they're always glad of volunteer help, even if just for a short while.' She paused. 'By the way, I got my posting today. It is going to be Southampton. I leave in a couple of days. I can't wait.'

Her eyes were full of purpose.

I'd be alone here in a day or two, but I could do it. I was sure I could.

We telephoned our parents, and the response was as expected. As I feared, my father would have come to London and would have insisted on bringing me home, but his gout was so bad, my mother informed me reproachfully, that he could not make the journey. She followed that with a list of reasons why I could not possibly stay on my own, but I surprised myself by standing my ground.

Mother's resolve weakened. She finally conceded and said, 'Well, maybe a few more days will do no harm. The daily woman will be there to keep an eye on you. I will telegraph Elizabeth Winterson and Lady Bridges to tell them that you are in London. Perhaps they could call on you.'

She added a whole list of dos and don'ts, and followed up the call with a letter containing an additional list. She also included the names and addresses of her friends, people on whom I could call in case of need. The letter made me smile; I could hear Mother's voice so clearly. I felt a small twinge of regret for the anxiety and worry I was causing my parents. But it was soon extinguished by anticipation and excitement. My humdrum life was behind me, for the time being at any rate. I was a free woman, and I felt my life was just beginning.

CHAPTER
Twenty-Five

The next couple of days were a whirl of activity. In between her own preparations, Margaret took me to the Red Cross headquarters to meet a lady called Miss Wentworth. She seemed to be in charge of the whole big building, which was a hive of busy people. She seemed rather distracted during our hasty introduction, but said that, yes, there was always lots to be done and every pair of hands helped.   'You're younger than your sister, aren't you?' Miss Wentworth asked that first morning.

I was rather surprised; I'd thought my age would be obvious, though, for some reason, I'd put my hair up that morning and worn one of Margaret's ankle-length skirts instead of my usual mid-calf one. I suppose I did seem older.

'Yes, a bit,' I said, neatly telescoping the actual eight years between us. It was nice, for once, not to be thought of as a child.

Miss Wentworth handed me the large pile of grey blankets she'd been carrying and said, 'Well, good for you, following in her footsteps. Always nice to see young girls volunteering for VAD service. You have your parents' permission, of course?'

She did not wait for an answer but picked up another pile of blankets and said, 'Follow me. I'll show you where to put them.'

'Oh, but—' I began, but she was already marching away down a corridor.

I stayed silent, pondering her words, as I spent the morning fetching, carrying, scrubbing dishes, counting supplies of sheets and pillow cases, running errands and doing whatever had to be done. I hadn't thought of following in Margaret's footsteps, but the seed had been planted and was growing. Could I be a nurse too? Remembering Edward and the wounded officers back home and what I'd seen of the nursing work there, I believed I could. Of course, there would be far more to it than reading to injured men, fetching them cups of tea and pushing them in bath chairs. There'd be blood, mess and hard work. But I could learn. I was young, strong and looking for a purpose. There was the matter of age, of course. Girls had to be eighteen to train as VADs and I wasn't yet quite seventeen, though my birthday was only weeks away. But lads joined up at sixteen or seventeen and went to war, so why shouldn't I? My mind was seething with new ideas. Suddenly, the future seemed to take on a whole new meaning.

There was no time to talk to Margaret of my thoughts. By the next day, she was gone, smart in her dark blue dress, white cap, apron and dark blue cape. The sight of the red cross on the front of her apron and cap brought a lump to my throat and strengthened my growing idea. We hugged and I even shed a tear as we said our goodbyes. We had grown genuinely close in the past week. I went back to the flat with renewed resolve and made my plans.

Miss Wentworth led me through the steps I would take. I had a twinge of conscience when she asked my age and I lied. I had another, bigger, twinge when, back at the flat, I took writing paper from my father's desk and wrote a letter of parental consent. There were papers with his signature in the desk and, after practising for some time, I did a fair imitation of it to end the letter. It was all surprisingly easy. The letter was read; it was accepted. I sailed through the interviews, quoting at one point my 'experience' of caring for convalescent soldiers at my home. What might happen if, or when, my deception were discovered, I pushed firmly to the back of my mind. In the space of a few short weeks, I was a trainee VAD.

*

I was rather nonplussed when I found that I was required to live at the Red Cross headquarters with other trainees for the duration. If I'd thought at all, I suppose I'd imagined I would be travelling each day to and from my father's comfortable flat. Instead, I found myself sharing a cramped room with several other girls.

I did not get off to a good start. I had quite a shock when I saw the accommodation: each of us had a curtained-off space, just big enough to hold a narrow bed and a small chest of drawers. I had another shock when I saw a girl at the next bed unpacking her case as I went in. She looked so like our former housemaid, Ada; she had wavy, fair hair and a cheeky expression.

She must have caught me looking at her because she closed her empty case, shoved it under the bed and said, 'Think you'll know me next time, then?'

I felt myself flush. 'Oh. I'm sorry for staring. It's just that you look like someone I know – our housemaid Ada, actually...' I tailed off, conscious that I was babbling.

She pulled a face. 'Oh, you're one of the posh ones! Thought as much, you can always tell. There's a lot of 'em here. But you'll find nobody puts on airs and graces; we all muck in together, *actually*.'

I didn't quite know how to reply. I said lamely, 'Well, it's nice to meet you. My name's Harriet.'

'Oooh, la-di-da! Posh name too! Wouldn't be *Lady* Harriet, by any chance, would it?'

She laughed. I felt my blush deepen, but she quickly seemed to relent. 'Only teasing, love! My name's Lizzie. Pleased to meet you.' She held out her hand and I shook it.

In the coming days, I found that Lizzie turned out to be a good-natured person who took me under her wing. She soon became a good friend and didn't turn a hair when she eventually discovered that I was, indeed, Lady Harriet. I found that several other trainees were of my class; we learned our craft alongside girls from factories and shops, and there were some who'd been servants in big houses such as Compton Manor.

Together, in our long, white aprons, caps and black stockings, we learned to make tightly tucked hospital beds, rolled miles of bandages and practised basic first aid, often on one another. With much hilarity, we put one another's arms and legs in splints, applied bandages and dressings to limbs and heads, and took one another's temperatures. We also learned to supervise the use of bedpans and to empty and wash them; to scrub floors, tables and utensils; to cook, clean and do all the jobs that Lizzie described as 'skivvying'.

We would be doing all these things, we were told by our instructor, so we mustn't think for a moment that we would just be smoothing pillows and stroking patients' foreheads. I was thankful again for the few housekeeping skills I'd learned in the kitchen at the manor, and even more thankful for the help and kindness of Lizzie, who tut-tutted over my shortcomings but was often there to pull me out of a sticky spot.

My hands grew rough and red from hot water, salt and carbolic soap. Lizzie came to my rescue with a pot of homemade hand cream: a mixture of oatmeal, garlic and lemon, which smelled strongly but did help. In the evenings, some of the girls still had energy enough to change and go out into London, but I was usually just thankful to wash, eat and then collapse on my bed and sleep.

My birthday came and went while I was in training. Cards and letters arrived for me at the flat, which I returned to now and then. I had told my parents of my intentions and was surprised that they had not reacted more forcefully. I think Mother had the idea that they were a passing fancy and that I would return home when I'd had my fill. Hugo was at the front, Mother and Papa said. They had not heard from Margaret since her posting. Had I? I knew that Margaret was probably far too busy to write letters, and I hardly had time for a quick reply myself. I hoped it would suffice. I was seventeen, I told myself, an adult person. By the time I had finished my training and received my certificate, I would be well on the way to following what I was increasingly coming to believe was my purpose in life.

CHAPTER
Twenty-Six

We were qualified Voluntary Aid Detachment nurses and we had received our first posting, at the same London hospital where Margaret had been. I eagerly looked forward to real nursing on real wards, containing real patients. In this, I was disappointed. Real patients there were on our ward, mostly recovering surgical cases, but our nursing ambitions were generally thwarted. Usually, we newly fledged VADs were kept busy with the more mundane tasks, such as scrubbing miles of corridor floors and scores of rubber sheets, not to mention the continuous succession of bedpans. We also washed huge piles of plates, cups and cutlery.

We had a little contact with patients when we made their beds, took hot drinks and meals to them or carried away their dirty crockery to the kitchens. We began to observe something of the horror of the injuries of warfare: the shattered or missing limbs, disfigured faces and terrible disabilities, although these men had been treated and were recovering. Perhaps this was the purpose of our first posting, to break us in gently to the things we would later have to face. But only occasionally were we allowed, in those first weeks, to attend to the patients ourselves, to dress wounds and replace bandages, to help the men to wash and perform their bodily functions, while remaining optimistic, cheerful and kind. The regular nurses tended to look down their noses a little at us and regard us as girls playing at being real nurses; maybe there was some validity to their views.

My parents and I had exchanged more letters. I was somewhat frustrated, as well as relieved, by their attitude. I knew quite well that they could descend at any time, declare my underage status and take me away.

But they did not seem to take what I was doing seriously, regarding it as akin to the first-aid classes being held in their village. My mother wrote:

We are glad you have found a way of feeling useful and being occupied. We have realised that this is as good a way as any of filling your time until things return to normal. Your father says that now the Americans have entered the war, it is only a matter of time before it is all over. Lady Bridges has said you have not called on her yet. Do you think you would be able to go on your day off? She would love to see you.

I shuddered at the thought of sitting in Lady Bridges' drawing room, sipping tea, with her questioning me and no doubt relaying information about my appearance and demeanour to my mother. I would definitely not be visiting, even if I had the time. I did go back to my father's flat, now and then, to pick up letters and sometimes even to enjoy the luxury of a proper bath.

It was summer when everything changed. Our ward sister had news for us one day. She had heard from a large hospital in Paris that there was a shortage of nurses there. Could any VADs be spared to go to help? On a voluntary basis, of course. Lizzie and I looked at each other. We were tired of the monotony and hard work here; any change would be a good one, wouldn't it? And Paris! The very name made our hearts beat faster. We were among the first to volunteer.

*

Before embarking, we were given several days' leave. I thought of going home but had the uneasy feeling that, if I did, I would never get away again, especially if my parents knew I was bound for France. I determined that I would write a letter just before leaving, so that I would have arrived in Paris by the time they received it.

Instead, I asked three other girls to spend the time with me at my father's flat; the three I had got to know best: Lizzie, Laura, whose father was a landowner and who was a country girl like I was, and Elsie, who came from a family of fishmongers. We squeezed in together, two in the big bed, one on a camp bed and one on the living-room sofa. We had a grand old time of it, creating cooking disasters in the kitchen, going out for walks round

London, sitting up late giggling, chatting and drinking cocoa. One evening, we went to see *Chu Chin Chow* at His Majesty's Theatre and arrived home late in a cab. The daily help tut-tutted a little but made allowances because we were heading to France to nurse the dear, brave lads. I did not pay a visit to Lady Bridges.

*

To say that I was seasick on the Channel crossing would be an understatement. For almost the whole of the time, I vomited, retched, struggled with nausea and dizziness and, at times, wished to die. In between, I sat weakly on a bench, leaning my head against the bulkhead, eyes closed. I was so glad that Lizzie, Laura and Elsie, and some others we knew, were there. Lizzie was not at all afflicted with seasickness. For the whole of the trip, she bounced about excitedly, looking at all the sights and sounds, coming back at intervals to offer me sips of water and relay bits of gossip she'd heard.

'My, you do look an odd colour,' she observed cheerfully on one of her visits. 'Funny, that. Some of the others are sick as well. Me? I'm fit as a fiddle. It's exciting! You sure it wouldn't help you to take a little turn around the deck?'

I groaned. I knew that if I were to move, I would be sick again, and my stomach was already empty of everything.

'I'll try and take a nap,' I said weakly.

I did doze a little, although I was always conscious of the motion of the ship and the slap of the waves. My mind wandered to the past months – the rigorous changes, the hard work, the long hours, the wounded men – and then slipped further back into the past. I was a child again; Emilie and I were racing each other on the smooth grass of the park at Compton Manor. She was longer-legged than I and could beat me easily. She dived into a patch of brambles and disappeared, hiding from me.

'Emilie!' I called.

'Who's Emilie?' said a voice at my side. Lizzie was there again, with a steaming cup in her hand.

I dragged myself awake. 'Oh, someone I knew once,' I said.

Lizzie thrust the cup at me. 'Ginger tea. I managed to wangle some. It's supposed to be good for seasickness.'

I took a sip and it stayed down. I had not thought of Emilie for a while but realised, with a pang, that I still missed her deeply, more than I missed my family – even Margaret. I had new friends, but they would never replace her in my heart.

'You're looking better,' said Lizzie approvingly. 'A bit more colour in your cheeks. That sleep done you good.' She sat down beside me on the deck, tucking her long skirts under her. 'I've been chatting to some of the other girls. Before we embarked, one of them heard there's a new sister on the ward we're going to. A bit of a tartar, by all accounts.'

I was beginning to take an interest and felt I might live again. I took another sip of the ginger tea and realised I felt hungry. I wondered what time it was. It was already evening, I guessed. I struggled to my feet, staggered and would have fallen had Lizzie not grabbed me.

'Steady on! You've been sitting there all the time and haven't got your sea legs.'

I never did get my sea legs. It must have been later than I thought. Land was in sight: a dark smudge that grew into buildings and a harbour. In no time at all, we were docking.

'Oh my!' said Lizzie. 'We're in France! Foreign parts! Fancy!'

There was a great hustle and bustle as we collected our belongings and were shepherded off the ship. My legs were strangely weak and wobbly but my stomach had, thankfully, settled. We were herded on to a train and squashed together tightly in a carriage smelling of stale, sweaty bodies and tobacco smoke. In spite of being all jammed together, most of us were tired out and slept fitfully, nodding awake whenever the train lurched a little. An elbow in my ribs finally awoke me fully and a voice hissed in my ear: 'We're here! Paris!'

Darkness had fallen; we groped our way from the train, clutching our luggage. Our harassed supervisor insisted it was just a short walk to the hospital, where we'd be fed and shown to our new accommodation. The thought of food and beds spurred us on.

It seemed a long walk but, at last, we reached the large, looming hospital building, where we, a rather weary and travel-worn group in VAD uniforms, were ushered into a lobby to await further directions. The familiar smell of disinfectant and carbolic soap filled the air.

Someone bustled up and said, 'They're busy tonight, but Sister will be here directly.' The woman started to move away before pausing for a moment to say, 'She'll be glad to see you.'

'Thank goodness they talk English,' whispered Elsie.

The hospital seemed very large and grand. We caught glimpses of hurrying nurses and porters guiding trolleys on which were swathed figures.

They won't expect us to work tonight, will they?' whispered one girl.

Someone else groaned. 'Oh, I hope not! I'm starving and I need to sleep.'

I realised suddenly how very empty I felt: empty and hollow and strangely light-headed. I'd had nothing to eat since our very early start. I swayed a little. The supervisor peered at me. 'Are you all right, Nurse Compton? You're not going to faint, are you?'

'No,' I said, although I wasn't at all sure. She sighed with relief. The day must have been a great responsibility. 'Ah, here comes Sister.'

A slender figure approached, followed by a nurse with a clipboard, their heels soundless on the tiled floor. They stopped beside us. 'Ah, our new contingent. I am so pleased to see you. We need you.' She shook hands with the supervisor. I felt the colour drain from my face. I recognised that voice. I'd heard its calm authority often enough. I felt my knees grow weak and my body begin to sway.

Lizzie grabbed my arm. 'You can't faint now!'

'Is someone feeling unwell?' asked Sister.

'Unfortunately, some of us have been seasick,' explained the supervisor, giving me a pull-yourself-together look. 'I'm sorry, Sister.'

Sister said calmly, 'I'm sure you could all do with food and sleep. Let me just tick off your names.' She looked directly at me and I saw her give a slight start, from which she recovered immediately. Through a fresh wave of dizziness, which threatened to engulf me, I found myself looking into a pair of cool, grey eyes that I knew very well.

CHAPTER
Twenty-Seven

I could not believe it! Miss Grey – Abigail Grey – my former governess, now Sister Grey, serving in a hospital for soldiers returning from the front line! Hardly credible, but it must have been just as much of a shock for her to see a former pupil, in a Red Cross uniform, here in Paris. She recognised me too, although she made no acknowledgement of it. She merely wished us all goodnight and said she would see us tomorrow.

I pondered this turn of events, when I was in bed in the room I shared with two others, before falling into a deep sleep from exhaustion. Should I speak to her? Would she speak to me? And – oh, dreadful thought – would she reveal my true age?

It seemed not. The next morning, we were assigned our duties with crisp, clear instructions. The men we had nursed in London had sufficiently recovered to be able to make the journey home. Here, we began to experience the horror of seeing men fresh from the front lines and the full range of injuries they had sustained. Some of them were missing limbs and other body parts; some had been blinded and had terribly disfigured faces; yet others' lungs had been destroyed by mustard gas. These were men whose lives would never be the same. Here, we cared daily for those who were completely reliant on us, and we had to stay cheerful and positive in the face of the despair of many of them. They would need the most expert care before they could embark on the journey to convalesce in their own localities. Some would never see their homeland again.

Half-way through the afternoon, when I was told I could take a short break, I was called aside by Sister Grey. 'Nurse Compton, a moment, please.'

Lizzie, on the ward with me, gave me a sideways look. 'Golly, have you gone and done something you shouldn't, already?'

Sister Grey led me to a small storeroom and closed the door. 'Harriet, I could hardly believe it was you! But it is. Just taller! I'd no idea you were a nurse! I've often thought of you. How is your family?'

I gave her a brief outline of what I knew of my family members, all the while terrified that she would mention my age and send me packing. I hoped and prayed she would forget that I was still months away from my eighteenth birthday. Maybe she forgot or chose to overlook it but, whatever the reason, she never mentioned it. All of a sudden, she was the Miss Grey I had known and loved.

She asked after Emilie, which gave me a fresh pang, and said, 'She was such an outstanding pupil.'

And then, as if a switch had been flipped, she turned into Sister Grey again, cool and detached. 'Well, Nurse Compton, I wish you good success with us here.' She paused and then added, 'But please don't expect any preferential treatment from me. I shall regard you as I regard all my nurses. Go back to the ward now.'

I almost said, 'Yes, Miss Grey,' but caught myself in time. I replied, 'Yes, Sister.'

I was quizzed later about the conversation. 'Did you get a wigging?'

'No,' I said. 'She just knew my family years ago, that's all.'

And that was as much as I was going to say.

*

We slipped into our new routines; the days sped by, turning into weeks and the weeks into months. We reached December before we knew it. We nurses speculated over whether any of us would go home for Christmas. It didn't seem very likely. Some of the injured men were even more keen on the idea, especially the British Tommies.

'Back to Blighty in time for the old Christmas pud, d'you reckon, nurse?' asked one of them, Corporal Banks, as I changed his dressings one morning. I forced a smile and said, 'Maybe, if you behave yourself.' But, inwardly, I knew there was no chance. Gangrene was spreading through his body and I knew he would never leave the hospital.

Sometimes we young nurses wept together, usually in the sluices, where tears on our faces would be less noticeable.

'I can't stick it any longer. I really can't,' said Elsie one particularly bad morning when we had lost three boys during the night. I did not know whether I could either. But stick it we did. Our world was now within these hospital walls: the wards, the routines, the hard work, the griefs and the sorrows. The patients and the nursing and medical staff were now our family.

Christmas came and went. We decorated the ward with paper streamers; there was Christmas dinner for those who could eat it. We sang carols and wished one another a merry Christmas. There were letters and packages from home, which came to us as messengers from another world.

I had written to my parents regularly from Paris, and had been surprised at their responses and my own. It seemed almost as if they had given up their troublesome fears for me and had accepted that I had found where I belonged. I realised, for the first time in my life, that they were proud of me! I almost wept when that realisation came. I had always thought that I was not really wanted, that I was an unfortunate late addition to a family already complete. I had reacted with stubbornness, rebellion and deceit.

In a burst of remorse, I confessed my lies, my forgery of my father's signature and my manipulations; I asked for their forgiveness. My mother replied:

My dear child, we forgive you with all our hearts because we love you. We ask you to forgive us for our lack of understanding of your nature. We see that you are now fulfilled and have found a purpose in life. We are proud of you.

Tears filled my eyes as I read, but I had to laugh at her postscript:

Please do make sure you get enough sleep, and try not to get wet feet. I enclose the remedy Nanny always used when you had coughs or colds.

The New Year came, with uncertainty about what it might bring. Despite the Americans coming to our aid, there seemed no hope of an end to the war.

*

What the New Year did bring to the hospital was a new, young, British doctor. Dr Parker had apparently just qualified as a specialist in facial injuries. How he had avoided the services, we did not know; there was talk of his being a 'conchie', although that was mostly gossip. We later learned that he had, indeed, served at Ypres, where he had lost several fingers, which meant that he could no longer use a gun.

The nurses were all of a twitter. 'Isn't he just gorgeous?' said one. 'Like Henry Ainley in *Sweet Lavender*! And so clever. He can do more with his few fingers than most can do with ten!'

'And never too busy or full of himself to say hello, even to us VADs!'

'That wavy hair! Don't you wish you could run your fingers through it?'

Dr Parker was certainly handsome. He had an athletic figure and hair like burnished bronze. We speculated about whether he was married.

Laura was jubilant when she found that he was not. 'Do you think I might be in with a chance?'

We quickly brought her down to earth.

'I reckon he's a bit sweet on our Sister Grey,' said Elsie. 'Notice the way he looks at her? He's smitten with her, I swear.'

'Not a chance there, then,' said Lizzie. 'Not with the Ice Maiden. He won't get far with Sister Frosty Face.'

We all jumped as a clear, cool voice called from the corridor. 'Nurses, there's a lot of chattering going on! Step lively with those bedpans. Patients are waiting!'

We looked guiltily at one another, praying that we hadn't been heard.

I took particular notice the next time Dr Parker and Sister Grey did a round of the ward together. He did seem particularly attentive, bending his burnished head towards her dark one as they looked at charts and compared notes. Her usual calm, aloof demeanour did not change. 'Ice Maiden' did seem particularly fitting for her. Whatever happened – tragedies (and there were many), anxiety, long hours of work, the relentless pressure of too many calls upon her time – she remained calm and in control. And she never singled me out or acknowledged me in any way, except with regard to work.

And then a day came when everything changed.

CHAPTER

Twenty-Eight

Out of the blue, I received a message that Sister Grey wanted to see me in her office. We were exceptionally busy that morning; another convoy of men had arrived during the night. I entered to find her sitting at her desk, her usually pale cheeks ashen, her eyes enormous and full of something that looked like unbearable pain. She said, in a voice strangely unlike her own, 'Ah, Harriet. Sit down, please.'

I perched on the edge of the only other chair in the room, overwhelmed by a sense of foreboding. What had happened? And why was I suddenly Harriet and not just Nurse Compton? It must be something personal – to me… or to both of us.

She took a deep, shuddering breath. 'As you know, a new contingent has arrived. Some have gone into the officers' ward. I took a look at the list. One of them – I'm sorry, Harriet – but one of the acute cases is your brother.'

I felt myself stiffen. Sometimes, in the busyness of our lives and the pressured world of the hospital, I would go for days without thinking of my family. I'd almost forgotten that Hugo was serving here in France.

I said, 'Oh! Is he – is he badly hurt?'

She nodded. 'Very badly.' She paused, and I could swear I saw the glint of tears in her eyes. 'He has lost a leg and has some internal injuries. But the most worrying is the injury to his head. He is unconscious and, so far, has been unable to respond in any way. Of course, it's early days, but there is no guarantee that he will regain consciousness.'

I swallowed. Hugo and I had never been particularly close but I felt a deep pang of pain and apprehension. 'Can I see him?'

She nodded again. 'Yes. But you'll find it a shock. I'll go with you, if you like. We'll go tomorrow. There's just so much to do today, with the new arrivals.'

She had tried to prepare me, but I was shocked afresh when we did see Hugo the next day. I had become used to men in all kinds of conditions: groaning and crying out in agony; delirious and raving with fever; horribly mutilated so their features were hardly recognisable; possessing wounds that stank and suppurated, and that required all one's will power to dress. Hugo was and had none of these things. I noticed at once that one leg was gone below the knee, but the rest of him was swathed in bandages. His head was particularly heavily bandaged. One eye was covered; the other closed. His face was as white as the bandages and he was completely motionless. I thought of my tall, dashing, handsome brother and my eyes filled with tears.

'Can I speak to him?'

'We are not sure if he can hear. Or even see with the undamaged eye. We keep trying to communicate, but he did not come round after the anaesthetic. He has not shown any sign of responding. But we must keep trying. And praying.'

There was a tremor in her voice.

I spoke to my brother and touched his hand. There was no response, either from the broken body or the damaged mind.

Sister Grey touched my shoulder. 'Let's go now. You need to be back on duty. But we will have a cup of tea first.'

Over tea in her tiny room, I had questions I needed to ask. 'Will he... get better?'

She could not answer, but a look of utter desolation crossed her face. Seeing it, I spoke more boldly than I would normally dare to her. 'I always thought you didn't like him.' Then I could have bitten my tongue.

She looked at me and put down her teacup, which rattled a little in the saucer.

'I didn't always like him, it's true.' Then she added, very softly, 'But I think I came to realise – gradually at first – that I loved him.'

Another shock. I put down my own cup. 'But… you were always so cold to him.'

She looked at me. 'Yes. I had to be. I knew I meant nothing to him, no more than just a casual distraction, a light flirtation to pass the time. I had to distance myself. And then I was dismissed, accused of leading him on.'

I was appalled. 'I never knew that. I'm so sorry.'

She quickly pulled herself together, realising she had let down her guard for a moment. 'Oh, I'm sure it was all for the best. We couldn't really go on as we were. I've long forgiven the injustice. One has to, to gain peace.'

I fully understood, having so recently come to a place of peace with my family.

'And what now?' I asked, hardly believing that I was daring to speak to the dreaded Sister Grey in this way.

'Now,' she said slowly, raising her head to look at me, 'now, I shall do all in my power, night and day, to help him pull through. I will try to get transferred to that ward. If not, if I can't nurse him myself, I will be at his side every spare waking moment. I will do whatever it takes. If it is within my power, if it is God's will, I will help him live again.'

She spoke with such passion that I knew it was the truth. I could see her love for my brother in every word, every expression, every gesture she made. I felt awed by it. And I believed her. If anyone could save my brother, it was Abigail Grey.

CHAPTER
Twenty-Nine

I could not help but marvel at the depth of devotion Sister Grey showed to Hugo. She had been unable to be transferred to his ward, but during every spare moment she had, she would be there, doing the small things for his comfort that nurses often had no time to do: holding his hand, bathing his forehead, adjusting his pillows. I visited him as often as I could myself, and once found Sister Grey sitting there, leaning forward, with her head pillowed on her arms across the foot of the bed, fast asleep. I wakened her quickly. It would not do for a disciplined ward sister to be found exhibiting such an undignified posture.

There seemed to be no change in Hugo. Day by day, he lay white and still, hardly stirring even when he was tended to. My visits were usually short ones. There seemed little that I could do to help him.

Sometimes, when a patient was clearly dying, they would send for the closest relatives. There seemed no point in Hugo's case, he got no better and no worse, and nothing could be gained by my parents' coming. I was greatly relieved. I did not think I could cope with the stress and strain of having them there, even for a short time. They had been informed of Hugo's condition and I wrote too, telling them he was receiving the best possible care and that I visited often. I did not mention Abigail Grey.

Sister Grey called me aside one day when I had just visited. She closed her office door behind us. 'Harriet,' she said. 'I've been speaking to Dr Parker, who, as you know, specialises in head and facial injuries. He advises that we talk to Hugo or read to him, so that he might hear our voices. Patients in a deep coma sometimes can hear, even if they show no sign. So could you do that when you visit? I will do so, of course, too.'

I suddenly remembered Edward, and how the sound of my voice had seemed to reach him and soothe him as nothing else could.

'Oh yes!' I said. 'I have a book of poems somewhere, I'll read some to him.' This idea lightened something inside me; it was a positive action to take instead of standing by helplessly.

'And, Harriet, could we pray together?' she asked. 'There is power in prayer, in asking God to be our help and strength.'

'All right,' I said awkwardly. I had prayed, on and off, mostly in moments of desperation, not knowing whether God heard or not. I was not sure I was worthy of his answering my prayers. But with Sister Grey, there seemed to be a confidence in God that was very deep and real, even in the midst of distress and pain. I realised suddenly that it was God who gave her that calm and peace, that made her the person she was. She prayed now, and I felt tension drain away with each word. And then she prayed for me, and I felt the tears come to my eyes.

'Thank you,' I whispered.

'Trust God, Harriet,' she said, 'He knows about our pain, for he gave his only son to die on the cross. Jesus is real, he loves you and he cares.'

I began to read to Hugo whenever I was with him. I felt rather foolish, for there was never any response, but I persevered. Sister Grey read too, mostly from the Bible. Sometimes I entered quietly and listened, the familiar words washing over me: *'though I walk through the valley of the shadow of death, I will fear no evil, for thou art with me: thy rod and thy staff they comfort me'.*

*

Spring was coming and, with it, rumours of a big, new offensive, maybe the largest since Ypres and Passchendaele. We braced ourselves for the arrival of convoys of more wounded.

In their time off, the other nurses got out and about a little, but most of my spare time was spent with Hugo. I'd noticed that when I read my poems, or Sister Grey did so from her Bible, the other patients sometimes listened.

'You have a lovely speaking voice, nurse,' one of the wounded officers told me one day. 'And so does that sister. Nice and clear and slow. Not like some of the gabbling ones that make you feel tired listening.'

Once again, I inwardly thanked Miss Grey for her careful teaching.

And then, suddenly, everything changed. There were fierce battles along the front and many casualties; the field hospitals and Casualty Clearing Stations were overwhelmed. More Red Cross services had to be sent; more doctors and nurses were needed. Lists were being drawn up of people to be deployed. We were called, one windy March afternoon, to a special meeting, to await new instructions and be attached to new units. Lists were read out of nurses to be transferred. My name was on the list and so was Lizzie's.

Since the time we'd spent together on leave in London, Lizzie, Laura, Elsie and I had formed a tight little group. We were all very different but, somehow, we had learned to value one another as individuals, differences and all. We had planned, when spring came and the dreary winter was behind us, to spend our days off exploring more of the city.

'Springtime in Paris!' Laura exclaimed, clasping her hands. 'Could anything be more romantic? Even with a war on.'

But those plans were not to be. Laura and Elsie would stay, while Lizzie and I embarked on what must surely be the greatest adventure yet. The thought gave me shivers of apprehension, but there was a sense of excitement too. We would be where the real action was.

I went to say goodbye to my brother on the day before we were to leave. There was a lump in my throat. I did not know if we would meet again. I held his unresponsive hand and told him that I was going to another hospital. I said that spring was coming, and that, at home, the hawthorns would be covered with creamy blossom, that primroses would be peeping out on the banks under the hedgerows. I told him that soon everything would be better and we would both be back home. I said I loved him. I had never said such a thing to any of my siblings before, but now I meant it with all my heart.

And, suddenly, there was a faint movement of the hand I held. Just a slight twitch of the little finger. Probably a nerve twitching, I told myself. I knew it happened. But as I looked at his face, the pale lips moved slightly and a word was spoken in no more than a whisper. Just one word: 'Hattie!'

That was all. He lapsed again into silence. But it was enough. I flew to find Sister Grey. When I did, I gabbled: 'He spoke! He said my name. He really did! He knew my voice! That's good, isn't it? Means he can hear and understand...'

Sister Grey tried to calm me, but she was almost as excited herself. She told me it was indeed good. It was a small sign, but it showed that, somewhere in there, was a mind that remembered and was capable of remembering more. It was a real indication of hope for more improvement. She hurried off to find the doctor and relay the news.

So it was, when we set off at first light the next morning, I went with a fresh seed of hope germinating in my heart.

CHAPTER

It seemed a long, bumpy journey as we left the Paris streets and suburbs, and headed out into the French countryside. Six of us VADs, squeezed together, rode in the back of one of the Red Cross vehicles returning from the last convoy. It had been a very early start and we dozed a little, only to be jerked to wakefulness every time the lorry hit a very large bump or pothole in the road. From the glimpses we had of our surroundings, and when we stopped for a few minutes to stretch our legs, we noticed the faintest hint of new green buds on bare tree branches and, once or twice, a froth of pink blossom on a cherry tree. But everything changed as we drew nearer to the battlegrounds where the trenches were. We began to see bombed shells of buildings, blackened stumps that had been trees and bare fields where, by now, crops should have been planted.

In the afternoon, we arrived at the hospital that would be our new workplace. It was, we had been told, a kind of halfway point between the Casualty Clearing Stations and the larger hospitals, where the men would go when the injuries needing the most urgent attention had been treated. What we expected, I don't know, but the reality was much bleaker than anything we could have imagined. Long rows of drab huts were the wards, standing in what appeared to be a sea of mud, although it had not rained for a day or two. Other huts – our sleeping quarters, kitchen and canteen, and latrines – clustered nearby, connected by paths of duckboards. A chill wind blew as we climbed out of the lorry and stretched our cramped limbs.

I felt Lizzie shiver. 'Dear goodness! This must be the end of the world.'

I was inclined to agree. Nurses and orderlies were hurrying from hut to hut, faces set and intent. From somewhere not far away, we heard a dull rumbling that sounded like thunder, with an occasional, louder 'crump'. The hurrying people took no notice.

'Guns!' whispered one of the other nurses. 'It's the front! We're that close!'

We were greeted by the sister-in-charge, Sister Blake, a middle-aged, small, bustling woman who couldn't have been more unlike Sister Grey.

She looked us new arrivals up and down. 'You all look very young. You can't be much over twenty.' She looked at me as she spoke and I wondered if I was meant to reply. But she was already walking ahead of us to our quarters and did not seem to expect an answer. I breathed a sigh of relief. What would happen if she discovered I was only seventeen? But then another thought came. I wasn't seventeen any longer. My birthday had come and gone, and I hadn't even noticed.

'Food will be available in the canteen when you're ready,' said Sister Blake, and she left us to settle in. Our quarters seemed none too comfortable, bare and drab, and on the draughty side. The six of us would be sharing. Our narrow beds were laid out with blankets and pillows and sheets, ready to be made up. We shoved our belongings under the beds and set to, shaking out the blankets gingerly, glad that at least the sheets were clean.

'I bet these haven't been washed lately,' said one girl, Violet, sniffing cautiously at her blanket.

'As long as there aren't any fleas,' said one of the others.

Lizzie and I pulled faces at each other. For a sensible, practical person, Lizzie had a horror of anything small, alive and moving – fleas, spiders, wasps or mice. She couldn't understand how a posh girl like me could abide them.

'Can I move my bed a bit closer to yours?' she asked, with a shudder.

We had an unremarkable meal at the canteen, were taken on a brief tour of the other buildings and retired for the night, exhausted. We had been told that things were quiet at the moment but that a new intake of wounded men was expected at any time.

The rumble of warfare went on intermittently all night. We saw the occasional flash of gunfire light up the dim horizon. Strangely, we soon fell asleep despite all this.

What disturbed our slumber was a sudden shriek from Lizzie's bed.

'Oh! There's a rat in here! Listen!'

Sure enough, a scratching sound was coming from a corner of the room, next to a bed occupied by a girl called Kate. She added her own shriek to Lizzie's. 'It's after my cake – the one I brought with me. Blooming cheek!'

We had been told to keep all foodstuffs – cake, sweets, chocolate – in tins, but Kate had obviously forgotten. She leapt from her bed, seized one of her work shoes and flung it forcefully at the sound. There was a squeak and then silence.

'Got him!' said Kate. 'Look!' We saw, in pale moonlight, that she was triumphantly holding up a small mouse by the tail. Lizzie was having hysterics; it took a while to soothe her, even after the mouse had been flung outside and we had all gone back to bed. But we managed to fall asleep again.

We began our work on the wards the next day. There was a small operating theatre attached to the hospital, where emergency treatment – amputations of injured or gangrenous body parts, or other life-saving surgery – could be carried out before the men were moved on to a larger and better equipped hospital. Most of the ones we treated on our first two days seemed reasonably stable, in need of careful nursing but out of immediate danger. We had time to chat with them, to encourage those who were despondent and to write letters home for those who could not. Fresh from the trenches and their horrors, the lads were often pathetically grateful for our care, and the sight of pretty young nurses their own age seemed to help dispel some of the horror.

And then everything changed. A convoy of patients had been dispatched, leaving empty beds to be freshly made up and waiting. An air of expectancy filled the camp; the guns had rumbled incessantly for days, with hardly a pause.

And then came the wounded: dozens of men with grey faces, men covered in caked blood and mud, whose rank was often indistinguishable; men with limbs shattered or missing, men with the most grievous internal injuries. Many would not survive. For those, the most the medical staff could do was try to comfort them, to relieve the pain and to let them know that someone cared.

Everyone was needed, even the VADs, who were suddenly given responsibilities equal to those of regular nurses. I was assigned to a silent young man, deposited on a rubber-sheeted bed, one arm hanging from a shattered shoulder.

'He has internal injuries too, I'd say,' said Sister Blake briskly. 'Notice the pallor and sweating? You'll need to remove his clothing, ready for the doctor. Cut it off, there's no other way.'

She disappeared.

I fetched a pair of sharp scissors and bent over the young man. 'Hello, my name's Harriet.' I thought how foolish I sounded, as though I were introducing myself at a social function. 'I'm a nurse,' I went on. 'I'm going to be looking after you today. What's your name?'

His lips moved. I heard, faintly, 'It's Gary – Ginge.'

His hair was so streaked with mud that I could not tell its colour, but I supposed he was a redhead. 'All right, Ginge,' I said. 'I'm going to have to cut your clothes off. I'll try not to hurt you.'

I snipped away at the tunic and the vest underneath, both stiff and rank with sweat; he could not have changed for weeks. When I got to the injured shoulder he shouted with pain 'Stop! Stop!'

I felt sweat trickle between my own shoulder blades. 'Sorry – I'll try to be gentle.'

The shoulder was smashed; a bloody mess of flesh and splintered bone. I placed a clean cloth over it. His belt, trousers, puttees and underwear came off with a great deal of difficulty; he was conscious enough to be embarrassed and I tried to reassure him, covering him with another cloth. There was bruising and swelling to his abdomen: a sign of internal injuries. The boots were horribly hard to remove; fortunately, Sister Blake came by to check on me and helped. His socks were black and sodden; the pale flesh of his feet indicating trench foot.

'His toes seem all right though. No gangrene,' said Sister.

The smell of the man and his clothes were nauseating, but when we had him stripped and covered, Sister Blake said, 'Well done, Compton. Put a blanket over him. He'll be in shock and will need warmth.'

'Will he live?' I asked uncertainly.

'Depends on the internal injuries,' said Sister Blake. 'We've done all we can for him for now. Come along, others need us.'

There was no time to linger over each wounded man. All day we ran from patient to patient, blotting out the horrors, drawing on all our training and past experience. We needed every resource we had and more besides. There were several times, that day, when I found myself, almost without thinking, whispering under my breath, 'Help me, God. Oh God, help me!'

CHAPTER
Thirty-One

We fell into a routine, of sorts. The wounded came in waves, after battles that were being fought all along the Somme. When they came, the pressure was relentless. We worked from dawn to dusk, unless we were on night duty, which, in some ways, was even more distressing: there were often deaths in a ward full of men crying out in pain or raving with delirium. For the ones who managed to sleep, there were frightening nightmares. We went from bed to bed, calming the distraught, giving morphine to those in pain, rearranging dishevelled coverings, trying to reassure those whose nerves had gone. Only rarely did we have a night without a serious disturbance. After one such night, Sister Blake took me aside and said, 'You did well, Compton. I recommend you take training as a regular nurse when all this is over.'

I went back to our quarters in the chill light of dawn, tired to the bone but glowing with the praise. Over to the west of us, the rattle and boom of gun and shell fire heralded the start of a new day of conflict. Even now, I thought, boys will be facing the day by going 'over the top'; for many, it would be the last time. For every one that might end up, broken and helpless, here with us, there would be many who never saw another dawn. I found myself praying often these days, and I prayed now, silently in my mind: 'Oh God, end this! Stop this killing!'

Yet strangely, I was not unhappy. I was doing my part. I was making a difference.

We had our time off, of course; we could not have managed without it. Once or twice, some of the girls and I had walked through the woods into the village, braving the possibility of lurking snipers. We even had coffee at one of the little shops. We were stared at curiously by the local people, but they respected the red crosses on our caps and were kind, although there was war-weariness on every face. Mostly, though, we spent our time off duty washing our clothes and our hair, and were glad when we could dry both outside in the warm summer weather. Lizzie's fears about fleas – among other things – had been realised; we tried our best but body lice were persistent, hiding in the seams of clothing, and bed bugs bit at night. No amount of sprinkling with Keating's Powder seemed to deter them. There were rats, too, lurking about; we had all learned to keep foodstuffs well protected. Letters and postcards came sporadically from home, often delayed. I'd had a brief note from my sister Margaret; she was now nursing at a hospital in Belgium.

I had a week's leave towards the end of summer, and I wondered if I should go home. But the thought of the wearisome journey, the seasickness, the very brief time there before having to travel back all deterred me. I could hardly imagine what my old life had been. So I went to Paris and found lodging near the hospital. My brother was still there and so was Sister Grey, faithfully caring for him in every spare moment. She greeted me formally in front of the others, but warmly when we had a moment alone in her little office. 'It's so good to see you, Harriet. You're thinner. Hugo is so much improved!'

He did look better, though still a shadow of his former self. He continued to have long periods of unconsciousness. Sister Grey told me there was shrapnel lodged in his brain and that possibly surgery could be done when he was more stable. The outcome was uncertain. But he had lucid moments, as I found when I visited. He recognised me and said, 'Hattie! Little Hattie, what are you doing in this place?'

I held his hand and talked to him quietly. He was not entirely sure of his surroundings: at times, he thought he was in a munitions factory; at others, that he was in a science laboratory and that he was being experimented on. He knew Sister Grey, however, and trusted her, though he sometimes referred to her as Nanny. But it was all good progress, I was told.

I went away cheered to catch up with Laura and Elsie, who insisted on showing me some of the sights of Paris: the Eiffel Tower, the magnificent cathedral of Notre Dame, and Montmartre. I also relished several nights of uninterrupted sleep, and the luxury of a hot bath and scented soap.

I returned, refreshed, to find an air of suppressed excitement among the other VADs. Kate had departed on leave and a new recruit, Isobel, had come to take her place. Isobel was one of the 'posh' girls, as Lizzie described them, a little older than the rest and rather superior.

'She looks down her nose at us commoners,' Lizzie told me gleefully, when we had a few moments alone. 'Grace and May are all right to mix with, but me and Violet are like a bad smell under her nose! She wanted your bed, as its nearest the window, but I told her she couldn't because my friend *Lady* Harriet would be back soon. Her mouth fell open! Stuck-up snob!'

But Isobel wasn't the only newcomer. There had been a new intake of wounded, and one of them was a prisoner of war, a *German*! The others were all a-twitter.

'He was picked up in the woods, covered in mud and nearly dead!'

'Sister gave us a talking-to. Said we're not to think of him as an enemy, just a wounded man, that the Red Cross treats *all* wounded men the same.'

'But he's a *German*! Think of having to touch him, wash him, change dressings!' Violet shuddered. 'I hope she doesn't ask me to. Wouldn't it just make your skin crawl?'

For some reason, the thought of Emilie came into my mind. I remembered our holding hands as we ran across a field of clover, making daisy chains and arranging them around each other's necks, and putting our heads together over a game. She was German: I'd touched her often; my skin hadn't crawled. Why should it?

We had twisted our hair together and vowed to be friends and sisters for ever.

'You're quiet, Compton,' said Grace. 'What are you thinking about it?'

'I think,' I said, 'that Sister Blake is right. A wounded man is a wounded man. We treat him just like all the others.'

Violet was persistent. 'But a *German*! We all know what they do. They kill babies with bayonets and slaughter whole villages, old people and all! Fair makes my flesh creep!'

'I'm tired,' I said. 'I'm on the early shift.' I lay down and pulled the blankets up high, trying to shut out the chatter.

As it turned out, I was detailed to care for the POW the very next day. He was at the end of the ward, curtained off from the others. His head had been shaved – because of lice, I imagined – and his cheekbones stood out in a pale, gaunt face. He had not eaten for days before he was found, I'd been told, and even now had to be fed every mouthful as he could not move his arms. He had a spinal injury and was in a great deal of pain. His other injuries were healing, but he would need surgery to remove the shrapnel, if it were possible. His eyes were closed and he looked pathetically young.

I put down the soup I carried. 'Hello,' I said 'I'm Nurse Compton. I've brought your lunch.' Then I bit my lip. Maybe he didn't understand English. I racked my brains for the German I'd learned from Janina. '*Hallo. Ich bin eine Krankenschwester. Mein Name ist* Nurse Compton.'

His eyes flew open and I saw that they were blue-grey and full of pain. He said in a hoarse whisper, '*Sprechen Sie Deutsch?*'

I floundered, the German words going out of my head. 'Not very well, I'm afraid.'

He said, 'That is all right. I speak a little English.' Even those few words seemed to exhaust him. I picked up the bowl and spoon. His face twisted, but he opened his mouth obediently. I fed him a few spoonfuls, as if I were feeding a child.

He swallowed painfully and then turned his face away. 'Enough,' he said, then added, '*Danke.*'

'Are you in much pain?' I asked. Beads of sweat were standing out on his forehead. Even the slight motion of swallowing a few mouthfuls had caused him agony. I felt a sudden wave of pity. He was a boy, who was, I guessed, a year or two older than I was – a boy wounded and a prisoner in enemy hands. Had his family been informed of his wounding and capture? His pain seemed to be intense. He gasped and pleaded, forgetting his English, *'Bitte, Fräulein, bitte...'*

I pushed back the curtain and went to find Sister. She was brisk but not unfeeling. 'That shrapnel is pressing on spinal nerves. It must be agonizing. I'll see what I can do. You collect the lunch trays from the others.'

I could not get the young man out of my mind. His rank and name, they said, were Gefreiter Bernhardt Meyer. It was my duty at times to tend him, wash him, dress his wounds, turn him and feed him. The pain I must have caused never brought more than a whimper, but sweat stood out on his forehead and he sometimes bit his lips until they bled.

'They don't feel pain like we do, the Hun,' remarked Isobel one day, as we washed bowls together in the kitchen. 'They're not the same as us.'

I could have slapped her. But I just picked up a pile of clean bowls and walked away without a word.

CHAPTER
Thirty-Two

Lizzie returned from her week's leave buzzing with excitement. 'The war's not going to last much longer! The Yanks are here at last! I seen them. Rows of them, marching away from the railway station! Great, big, strong chaps, smart as paint! It won't be much longer now, you'll see!'

Her picture of the American soldiers – such a contrast to the weary, muddy, war-sick French and English we saw here, even the ones not wounded, taking their brief respite from the trenches – put heart into everyone. But autumn was here, the leaves were falling and it rained, turning the ground once more into a quagmire. We tried to keep to the duckboards as we passed among the buildings, but even so, the hems of our dresses were continually muddy and bedraggled. Morale was low at the prospect of winter. I had been told I could be posted to another hospital if I wished, but I chose to stay and so did Lizzie. Some of the VADs left; others came. In the acute ward, the POW developed a fever and, for a few days, his life hung in the balance. Infections were common: the strongest came through them; many did not. We silently mourned for those who would never see their homes again, but there were still the living to be cared for.

Even through fevered delirium and constant pain, Bernhardt was stoical. He was pathetically grateful whenever I bathed his head with cool water or administered his morphine. He murmured something one day, when the edge of the pain was beginning to wear off, and looked at me with fever-bright eyes. '*Ach*, you are an angel. *Mein Engel*!'

I started at the stab of a memory; the words were familiar. It was what Janina always called my mother. It was only a few short years since those days, but already they seemed an eternity away. I patted his hand gently.

His fever abated and there was talk of operating to remove the shrapnel and, it was hoped, relieve the pain, and perhaps even restore some movement. His strength had to be built up for the surgery, so he was fed beef tea and nourishing soups: the best that could be obtained.

'That Hun gets more pampering than our own lads.' I heard similar mutterings more than once among the nursing staff and other patients. A couple of them looked at me.

'And you seem to be the one feeding him, more often than not,' said one. 'Are you a bit sweet on him?'

The tone was sarcastic but I felt a flush rise to my cheeks. I didn't reply. There was a grain of truth in what had been said. I did volunteer for the task of giving Bernhardt his food whenever I could, and tending to his other needs. I liked him. He was so young, and so pathetically grateful to be shown kindness and that someone could speak his language a little.

We talked briefly, in German and English, smiling at our mistakes. He was a country boy, he said, and wondered if he would ever see home again. Like so many others, he had been keen to enlist but had come to see how futile it had been, man fighting man. He had reached the conclusion that his land would be defeated; he did not know what the future would hold. So many of his comrades had lost their lives. I thought of our own lads from back home: freckled Henry and Ben and Ernie from the village who would never return. I did not often cry but I had wept for Henry, who had laughed and teased us girls but had the kindest heart, for Polly and for the sheer waste of it all. I told Bernhardt that I was a country girl too.

'You have such a beautiful speaking voice,' he told me one day. 'Clear and gentle and soothing. It lifts my spirits.'

It was the second time I'd been told that; I silently thanked Miss Grey again for her persistent tutoring. I could almost hear her calm instructions: 'Speak each syllable clearly, Harriet. Feel each word roll off your tongue. Don't gabble and fall over your words.'

'I could read to you, if you like,' I offered. 'I have a book of Tennyson's poems with me. And a Bible.'

But a day or two later, when I brought my Tennyson in my apron pocket, it was to find his bed empty, the linen changed and neatly made up. My heart sank. 'Where is Bernhardt?' I asked the man in the next bed, afraid of the answer.

He gave me an odd look. 'The Boche? Gone to theatre, so I gather. Not that he's a bad chap, considering. Good manners and all that. Best of luck to him, I say.'

My heart rose again. I realised I wanted, more than anything, for Bernhardt to pull through. I wanted to sit and talk with him; to tell him, maybe, of my childhood with Emilie – memories so precious and painful that I'd never spoken of them to anyone. I knew he would be interested that Emilie was a German girl. He seemed interested in everything, and I knew that, despite the disillusionment and the fact that he was a prisoner, he wanted to live. As soon as I had a break, I hurried back to my quarters and prayed earnestly for Bernhardt until I went back on duty again.

Bernhardt survived the operation. The doctors were cautiously optimistic that it had been successful. He was already beginning to recover a little of the movement in his hands and arms. He was still in much pain, but it was a different kind of pain. The result looked good, though he would need careful nursing for a long time. A flood of relief and joy took me by surprise.

He was impatient with his weakness, but utterly grateful for the skill of the surgeon. 'And for you, *mein Engel*,' he added. 'You have helped me so much. I will be eternally grateful.'

I read to him, both from Tennyson and from the Bible.

He said one day, 'You know, I had lost my faith in God but I am beginning to believe again, from the kindness I have been shown.'

I felt humbled. My own faith had been growing. I had confessed to God my own need for forgiveness and for the grace of Jesus Christ in my life. It did not change anything outwardly but, gradually, I began to feel the assurance that, in all the turmoil of life, I was not alone.

And then the blow fell. I was summoned to the matron's office one day, and found both her and Sister Blake there. I looked from one face to the other. Both had stern expressions.

141

'Nurse Compton,' said Matron, who was reckoned throughout the hospital to be formidable but fair. 'It has been brought to our attention that you have been spending a great deal of time with a patient.' She paused. 'In fact, an enemy patient, the POW Gefreiter Bernhardt Meyer.' There was another pause. 'Now, you must know that these friendships between nurses and patients are strongly discouraged. In fact, we take a very dim view of them. Relationships in wartime can be disastrous. Many of these men are married or attached. And when the patient is an enemy POW, it cannot be overlooked. Fraternization with the other side is strictly forbidden.'

'I wasn't fraternizing!' I burst out. 'And he isn't married…' My voice tailed away. I didn't know whether he was married or not.

Matron held up her hand. 'But you have been spending undue time with him while on duty and visiting him during your off-duty hours. Such conduct cannot go unpunished. Discipline must be maintained.'

My heart was thudding. 'What – what will happen?'

'You will have no further contact with this prisoner, either on or off duty. And – I regret having to do this, as you have proved a very promising nurse here – I will have to arrange for your transfer to another hospital as soon as it can be arranged.'

Her lips were set. I knew it would be of no use arguing. I was to be sent away in disgrace. I walked back to my quarters, skirts trailing in the mud, utterly devastated. To leave under a cloud was unbearable; it would probably end my career. And there was something even worse; a realisation that was a terrible stab to my heart: I would never see Bernhardt again. Then I knew that I had fallen in love with him.

CHAPTER
Thirty-Three

I told no one except Lizzie, when we had a moment alone together, and then I told her everything, even my feelings for Bernhardt. She was shocked, dismayed, indignant and sympathetic by turn. 'That's dreadful! But a bit romantic as well, don't you reckon? Love stronger than the barriers of war – ooh, it's like something you see at the cinema! But that mean old stick of a matron, sending you away... That means we might never see each other again! I've got a good mind to go and tell her what I think!'

'Don't!' I begged. 'Getting yourself in trouble won't help. It's my own fault, really. But oh – I can hardly bear it!'

I sat on the bed, twisting my handkerchief in my hands, though I had determined I would not cry. I felt the stubborn streak in me rise to the fore.

Lizzie noticed the change in my expression.

'What are you going to do?'

I got up. 'Well, for one thing I'm not going until I've said goodbye to Bernhardt.'

Grace came in then and I said no more.

I watched for my chance. A few days later, I sneaked into the forbidden ward when I knew that Sister would not be there. It was a quiet spell, when breakfasts and morning rounds had been completed; the doctors weren't expected for another thirty minutes. I slipped into Bernhardt's cubicle and pulled the curtains. He looked surprised to see me. My nurse's eye noticed that there was a new tinge of colour in his cheeks. His shorn hair had grown to a fair stubble and his face seemed a little less gaunt. He was getting better.

'Nurse Compton,' he said and smiled.

I put my finger to my lips. 'Ssh! I'm not meant to be here. I'm being transferred. I didn't want to go without saying goodbye.'

His face fell. 'But – where? Why?' He reached out his hand.   The nurse in me thought, 'He's moving his hands!' But the woman in me could only say, brokenly, 'I don't know. But I can't bear it – can't bear to leave you…' I felt the tears rising and blinked them back. The tinge of colour left his cheeks and his fingers touched mine.   'Oh, *mein Engel! Mein Liebling*…' He paused, then added quickly, 'Wherever you go, please know this. I love you. I will always love you. And when this is over, I promise I will find you again. If that is what you want.'

'I do,' I said. 'I love you too—'

Then, suddenly, it was as if the whole world had gone mad all over again. There was shouting from outside, followed by a tremendous clamour of sound: a clashing of what sounded like cutlery on tin trays; a thumping and banging of wood on wood and metal.

Bernhardt said, 'What is it? What is happening?'

I was just as bewildered. Had a stray incendiary bomb hit the hospital? Was one of the wards on fire? Had the guns been turned on us, despite the large Red Cross signs on our roofs?

'I'm going to see,' I said. 'I'll be back.'

He called after me, 'Be careful, *mein Liebling*!'

I ran out into the grey chill of the November morning. People were milling around, inside and out, some as bewildered as I; others were jubilant, with smiles on their faces. I was seized by Lizzie, who had run out of the ward she was working on. She was almost incoherent with excitement, cap askew on her fair curls.

'It's over! I told you it would be soon! The war's over! The news just came through! Harriet – it's over!'

I could scarcely believe it. But it was true. When the mad hubbub of those first jubilant moments had calmed a little, we noticed something else. There was no rumbling and cracking of gunfire from over the horizon. The guns were silent.

We learned that the German army had surrendered and that that the peace treaty had been signed this very morning at eleven. The eleventh hour of the eleventh day of the eleventh month. It was done.

It was a very strange day. After the first, heady moments, there was a feeling, not of jubilation at victory, but just profound relief that, at last, it was all over. We had to return to our tasks. There were still wounded men to be cared for. There would be more when the latest casualties came in, and there would certainly be wounded men from both sides hiding out in the woods and farmhouses. The work of the hospital was far from done; there would be a busy time ahead.

All day long, we cared for our patients: those who were rejoicing at our victory, those too sick to care and those for whom it had come too late. I was seized and hugged by the walking wounded; the bestowal of kisses was demanded by others. Try as they might, the ward sisters had difficulty maintaining order. I felt exhilarated, relieved, exhausted and bewildered by turn, and sometimes all at once. But one conviction stayed in my mind and sang a new and joyful song in my heart: Bernhardt loves me! Bernhardt loves me!

*

The following weeks were strange ones, similar to those preceding and yet different: no longer the continual knowledge of warfare just miles away; no more waves of the wounded after another big push; just a gathering in of the last to be wounded. The hospital was slowly preparing to wind down. Those who could be transferred were transported away; there were now empty beds that would, thankfully, never be filled. Daily, I expected to be sent away on one of the lorries, but nothing was said. Whether my superiors had forgotten my misdemeanour, whether they had chosen to overlook it or whether the threatened discipline no longer applied in the new and heady order of peace, I did not know. Perhaps they just hadn't had the time to arrange my transfer.

I did not go near Bernhardt again, but, inwardly, I hugged the thought of him to my heart like a joyful secret. He loved me; I loved him. And he was making good progress.

The day came when there was news, which came through Lizzie, who was as good at overhearing conversations as I had been as a child – how far away that seemed now! One morning, when the first frosts had whitened the ground, she told me, 'They've been wondering what to do with your Bernhardt. He's officially still a prisoner, but the war's over, so prisoners are to be sent home. They've decided that they will send him home from here. Seems like they've got the papers and everything. He's to go by lorry and then train.'

I felt my heart stop. 'But he's still very sick. He's in pain, not fit enough to travel. He can't even walk yet and he's very weak—'

'They're thinking of sending a nurse with him.'

'What? What nurse? It ought to be me! I'll go! I'll go and tell them—'

'Harriet—' Lizzie began to warn me, but I was not listening. Whatever they said, I wouldn't care, even if it meant having to give up my nursing career. They *had* to let me be the one to go with Bernhardt. They just had to!

I rushed off to find Sister Blake, who was trying to make sense of food deliveries for the ward. 'Sister,' I said breathlessly, 'I heard they're sending Ber— the German prisoner home. He will need a nurse. Please let me be the one to go with him! Please!'

She looked at me, dumbstruck. 'Nurse Compton, have you taken leave of your senses? You are already under disciplinary measures. Indeed, you cannot go with the prisoner! Matron would never allow it!'

'Then I'll ask her!' I said recklessly.

I searched until I tracked Matron down. She gave me an incredulous look, similar to Sister Blake's. 'I've never heard of such a request! It is none of your business, but if someone is needed to accompany the prisoner—'

I actually interrupted her. 'Someone is. He can't walk yet. He needs medication for his pain. He's very weak. Please, please let me go!'

Matron took off her spectacles and looked at me. 'I am disappointed in you, Nurse Compton. The reports I've heard of you have been good. You have shown a great deal of promise. But since your inappropriate conduct with that enemy patient, you seem to have lost all sense of duty and plain common sense. If someone goes with that young man, it will be a mature, reliable nurse or an orderly. I am responsible for you young nurses, and I would be derelict in my duty if I were to let you go into an alien country – a defeated, dangerous country – unchaperoned, with a young man, recently a prisoner of war. Words fail me! I could not look your family in the face. You seem to have lost your senses. I will be recommending your return to England as soon as it can be arranged!'

I wrung my hands. 'Matron, please, I don't care about my reputation—'

'Obviously not. But I care about it and about mine, and that of our organisation. Not another word! Go!'

I could not. Another idea, born of desperation, had come into my mind and I boldly spoke it. 'Matron,' I said. 'Bernhardt and I – we love each other. We want to be together. I could travel with him, couldn't I, if he and I were married?'

Part Four
Harriet And Emilie

CHAPTER
Thirty-Four

Harriet

We were married within a matter of days by the weary, grey-haired chaplain who had comforted so many on their deathbeds and officiated at so many burial services here. He seemed slightly bemused to be conducting a marriage ceremony between a young English VAD nurse and a bed-bound, young, German ex-prisoner of war. Sister Blake and Lizzie attended the ceremony, which was short and to the point. In all the bustle and confusion of the first few weeks of the new peace, nobody enquired about our ages or parental consent. I had telegraphed to my parents and Bernhardt had telegraphed to his family. It was done. We were man and wife, for better or for worse.

I felt a strange tumult of conflicting emotions: joy to know that I was inextricably bound to the man I loved; relief that the war was over at last; slight apprehension but mostly excitement about the future; regret that I would be leaving behind all that I had ever known; and deep grief and sadness over the futility and loss of the past four years.

The evening before we left, there was a funeral service at the small cemetery in the village nearby, led by the same grey-haired chaplain. It was the burial of one of our young patients who had died very suddenly and unexpectedly. There had been all too many such services, and we nurses were usually too busy with our living patients to attend. This time, I decided I would go, maybe as a kind of symbolic gesture of farewell to all the young men and their lost hopes and dreams, but also to the end of my life as I had known it until now. One of the orderlies, who was a musician, was called on to sound the last post at these occasions. I'd heard the haunting notes from a distance many times. On this occasion, as we stood at the graveside of a young soldier who should not have died, it held added poignancy. As I heard the music rise to its final, questioning note in the cold wintry air, I felt my eyes fill with tears. I blinked them away and hurried back to the hospital to try to sort out which belongings I should pack.

I did not shed tears either when it was time for Lizzie and me to say goodbye, although I felt a great weight of them heavy in my chest. Lizzie shed enough for both of us, embracing me fiercely and saying through her sobs, 'You're the best friend I ever had, even though you're a lady!'

I said, and meant it, 'You've been a wonderful friend to me too, Liz, and I'll miss you terribly!'

Other goodbyes were more restrained. Everyone, including Matron, wished me well, although I could see they had grave doubts about my chosen path. Bernhardt was loaded on a stretcher and on to the lorry that would take us to the station. An orderly went with us; he and the driver would transfer Bernhardt to the train. After that, we would have to depend on the kindness of station porters and anyone else willing to help, and trust that the trains would be running. I loaded up our luggage and, most importantly, the medical items that Bernhardt would need for the journey, then climbed in beside him. I looked back just once as we drove away, seeing a group of weary people, some with red crosses on their white aprons, standing in front of a collection of drab buildings in a sea of mud.

It was a cold morning, so Matron had kindly made sure we had extra blankets for the journey. Bernhardt looked pale and set, but his blue-grey eyes glittered and he was smiling. The stubble on his head was lengthening into a new growth of fair hair. He reached for my hand. 'I am so grateful to you, *mein Liebling*. For me, you have given up everything. I will do my utmost to be a good husband.'

'Just get well,' I said. 'Nothing else matters.'

And I meant it. I smiled a little, thinking of my mother and the way she had flung up her hands at my impetuous ways as a child. I thought of her bewilderment at my joining the VADs and volunteering to go to France. What she would make of this last, impulsive action I could not imagine. I knew it was possible that I might never see my family again or my old way of life. But I also knew, without a doubt, that I was someone who considered the world well lost for love.

I had prayed earnestly for a safe journey. I knew trains had been derailed and blown up while the war was on. How many lines were still in operation? How much disruption would there be? How much delay? We had to cross the border. Who knew what lay ahead?

But God answered my prayers. The journey seemed slow and uneventful. We received a few curious looks, but there were many curious things in those first weeks after the end of the war. We had papers if we needed them. We were mostly left alone. I gave Bernhardt his morphine and we both ate and drank a little from our provisions. After a while, Bernhardt slept and I dozed a little, too, to the slow clackety-clack of the wheels on the rails.

We both awoke at the same time when the train halted. We had come to the German border. We would need to stay the night nearby and get another train the next day. Bernhardt was white again with fatigue, but the railway staff were helpful. They carried him from the train, directed us to a boarding house not far away, and even took us there with Bernhardt on a trolley, obviously feeling pity for the wounded man and his young wife.

The boarding house lady was German, Frau Koch, and she couldn't have been more helpful, especially when she discovered that Bernhardt was a returning soldier and therefore a hero. Yes, she could take us in, and she even had a downstairs bedroom, with a fireplace. The friendly porters deposited us and our luggage and left.

Bernhardt was desperately tired and in need of morphine again. While I tried to make him comfortable, Frau Koch put up a small camp bed for me. She did not question our unusual status, but I was glad I had a makeshift wedding ring, given to me by one of the other nurses. I would not have liked her to think badly of me.

'I have hot soup and fresh bread,' she said. 'So many people are travelling. I try to stay ready for whoever comes. I will bring the food to you. And water to wash.'

'*Vielen Dank*,' I said in German. '*Wir sind sehr dankbar für ihre Freundlichkeit.*'

She seemed surprised that I spoke her language, and told me that she was fluent in both French and English. 'I am so glad for the end of the war,' she told me quietly. 'We are defeated, but God is with us still.'

Both Bernhardt and I were exhausted and, when we had eaten, it took all my strength to attend to him and to get him settled. I fell into the camp bed and was immediately asleep. Bernhardt woke only once in the night; when I had made him comfortable again, we were both asleep in minutes. I woke feeling refreshed, and Bernhardt had a tinge of colour in his cheeks again. Frau Koch brought us breakfast: hot coffee, bread and sausage. She had enquired about the trains and said there would be one this morning. She had even recruited a couple of men to help carry Bernhardt to the station.

I sensed a fresh purposefulness in my new husband.

'Could you get me some clean clothes, please,' he asked. 'I should like to be respectable when I meet my family.'

I looked ruefully at my own creased and crumpled garments and hoped that I would have time to make myself presentable too. I got Bernhardt fed, washed and shaved, and went to his bag for clean clothing. His uniform had long gone; the only proper garments he had were another pair of hospital flannel pyjamas. Shaking them out, I noticed a photograph at the bottom of the bag and picked it up. Bernhardt had so few personal possessions; this must have been among the items taken from the pockets of his uniform, and I was curious.

The photograph showed a backdrop of thickly forested mountains, with a group of people in the foreground. There was Bernhardt, straight and proud in his uniform, and so tall! I had not fully understood how tall he was, and realised with a shock that I had never seen him standing. A young lad stood next to him, looking up at him with admiration. On his other side stood a smiling woman who looked so proud that she could only be his mother. Next to her was another woman – I drew a sharp intake of breath. I knew her! Surely, surely, it was Janina! My eyes flew to the last person in the group: a tall, slender girl, whose hair gleamed in the sunshine.

Bernhardt heard my gasp. 'Harriet – what is it?'

I took the picture to him and pointed at the girl, my hand trembling.

'Bernhardt – who is that?'

He looked at it. 'Oh, that is my little cousin, Emilie.'

For a moment, the room spun. I clutched the back of a chair and couldn't speak.

Bernhardt was alarmed. 'Harriet! What is it? Are you ill?'

I gathered myself with an effort. I just could not believe what my eyes were telling me! Emilie – my Emilie – was Bernhardt's cousin! His mother was Janina's sister; when I looked closer, I could see the likeness. All of them lived together and we were travelling to join them.

I would see Emilie again.

I had to sit down and close my eyes for a few minutes before I could, haltingly, explain my shock and surprise to Bernhardt. He was dumbfounded. And then he laughed. He had not yet received his morning medicine, so I knew that he must be in pain. But the sound of his laughter was the most joyous and unexpected sound I had ever heard.

'Oh, my Harriet,' he said. 'This must surely be God at work! I remember that photograph being taken. My mother insisted we do it; one for her and one for me. A neighbour took them. And that boy, Klaus, was so envious that we let him be in it too.' He laughed again and I laughed too.

Frau Koch came rushing in, thinking some calamity had happened and we had lost our senses. And she was amazed when we explained, and then insisted that we should telegraph this new discovery to Bernhardt's family so that they would be prepared.

We had to return to the real world. This stage of the journey was a hard and tortuous one, filled with many stops and delays; a difficult day in a newly defeated and broken country. But all day long, I carried the new knowledge about Emilie in my heart like a wondrous and unexpected treasure.

We arrived at Bernhardt's village at last, exhausted again, aching and travel weary, our eyes gritty with tiredness. A car met us, sent by Bernhardt's family to carry us home. As we climbed into the mountains, I thought the scenery was the most beautiful I had ever seen, even in winter. Dusk had not quite fallen, and I saw majestic mountains rearing up to meet the sky, some already snow-capped. The air, clean, sharp and cold, was full of the scent of pine. Huddled in his blankets, Bernhardt seemed to gain fresh strength with every new turn of the winding road.

The family was waiting to greet us outside a farmhouse that looked like something from a fairy tale. There were Bernhardt's mother and Janina, who, I could see now, were unmistakably sisters. There was even the skinny boy, Klaus, eager and waiting to greet his wounded hero. And there, standing straight and still, as pale and graceful as one of the silver birches in the forests we had passed through, was Emilie, my Emilie. She was taller but still the same.

The women clustered round, advising the driver on how best to transfer Bernhardt from the car into the house. I did not wait for introductions; I scrambled from the vehicle and stumbled forward. Emilie came towards me, arms outstretched, and I felt myself enfolded. We did not speak but, at last, I let the tears flow.

CHAPTER
Thirty-Five

Emilie

Spring has come again, the second spring since the war ended. The valley is cloaked in a haze of green; the fruit trees are a froth of pink and white blossom; and the tiny fairy thimbles that I love are displaying their blue bells. The *Gasthaus* is beginning to be busy again and the farm, too, is bursting with new life. Our poor, defeated country is slowly, slowly, beginning to recover.

Benno returned and, with him, wonder of wonders, my Harriet. When we first heard the astonishing news of the identity of Benno's young wife, my feelings had been in turmoil. I could scarcely take it in. I had no idea that Harriet had become a nurse or that she had been working at the very front-line hospital to which Benno had been taken. I could not grasp how such a thing could have happened. But the sudden decision to marry had been so typical of the Harriet I had known and loved. Yet, a little later, a tiny flicker of resentment had crept in. Benno and I were cousins, but we had become friends too, friends and confidantes through the long letters exchanged between us. I felt our friendship was special. Surely, with a new wife, that would change. I had longed to see Harriet but, now, I was not sure that things could ever be the same between us.

I had held back when the vehicle carrying them had arrived. My mother and aunt were all agog, hardly able to wait to begin the care of the wounded hero. They had rushed to his side the moment the car stopped, eager to get their hands on him. I stood back, not quite sure of how I would greet Harriet or of how much she would have changed.

And then I saw her, emerging from the car, stumbling a little, her eyes deeply shadowed and her face grey with fatigue. She paused a little, uncertain, looking very small and vulnerable. But then she saw me and her eyes lit up, and she was my Harriet again. It was as if the years between fell away. I did not wait any longer but ran to meet her with open arms. I felt her tears wet against my cheek, mingling with my own.

*

Benno and Harriet have moved out now, to their own small, picturesque home, a little further down the valley. My mother says it reminds her of the place where she and my father lived, and where I was born. Benno grows stronger by the day. How could he not? He has this pure, clean air, good, farmhouse food and, most of all, the continual, tender care of his devoted wife.

I am amazed at the change in Harriet. Who would have guessed that the spoiled, capricious, headstrong, demanding child, who was also my dearest friend, would turn into this loving, caring, devoted, faithful young woman? She is determined that Benno will regain his full strength and, every day, we see the improvement. From a helpless, pain-racked wreck of a man, he has already become stronger and more confident: one who looks to the future and is determined to live and to walk well. He smiles and laughs. He has been able to use his hands more and more. He carves and whittles things from wood. He is sure that, one day, he will be able to do a full day's work again. And he and Harriet adore each other.

From the beginning, his mother or aunt, or sometimes both, have gone to sit with Benno in the afternoons, so that Harriet can have a change and a rest. Mostly, Harriet comes to spend the time with me. We take a walk in the woods or across the farmland, or, in wintry weather, we sit by a blazing fire and do some crochet or needlework. Now that Harriet expects a baby in early summer, we have been working on an ever-growing collection of baby clothes. Our friendship has grown stronger. We talk about the future, the present and often the past. At these times, the years slip away and we are little girls again, giggling together at some silly joke or planning a prank. We remember dear old Nanny and her little ways, and laugh about Louisa's lofty ambitions and Caroline's horsy passions.

Harriet hears from her family occasionally. Whatever their private feelings, they have swallowed their pride and been able to wish her well in her marriage. I think that her mother is mightily reassured that she has my mother here to support and help her when she needs it. Lord and Lady Compton also sent a considerable gift of money.

Harriet is rather pensive after a letter from home. She realises the pain and worry she caused by leaving home in the way she did, by joining the VADs and going to the front lines. But she has no real hankering to go back, at least for a while. Her life is here now and she is happy in it.

Her parents moved back into the manor house when the patients were discharged, and they live there now, in solitary splendour. Hugo and Abigail Grey are married and live at the lodge, where Abigail has nursed Hugo back to health with the same devotion that Harriet shows to Benno. I marvel at the two pairs, wondering if I could ever show the same level of devotion. Maybe I could if I loved someone. Perhaps, one day, I will meet someone I can love. They say that many women will remain unmarried because, across the length and breadth of the Continent, a whole generation of young men has been wiped out.

Louisa's army officer was one who did not return from the war. She married Archie Davenport, who had been exempted from service because of a hearing disability; she has her own house and servants. Caroline is married too, to a man much older than she is; he's the owner of a prominent racing stud farm. She must be in her element. Margaret has stuck to her vow never to marry. She came back from nursing in Belgium and now works as a nurse, midwife and trusted confidante among deprived, downtrodden women in the East End of London. Her dream of equal rights for women has borne some fruit; women over the age of thirty now have the vote.

A few of the servants remain at the manor. Most of the young men did not return and many of the young women now have other work.

As for me, I plan to travel, to explore the unknown parts of my country and maybe to venture into other European countries, to see how they are faring in this new world. They say that the war was a war to end all wars; I pray that it is true. I have a hankering to go to Herefordshire, to see the rich, red soil of the parkland and rolling fields, and perhaps to visit the Compton family. I could take them news of their daughter. But I will stay until after the birth of Harriet's baby.

I plan to write about everything I encounter in my travels. I will write about the places I see, the people I meet (their thoughts, feelings and hopes for the future), the countryside I pass through, the climates I experience, the architecture of the cities and the devastating effects of the war. With regard to my own emotions, hopes and dreams, I may be in for a great many disappointments, hardships, surprises or shocking discoveries. There may be times when I wish I had stayed safely at home with my family. I may learn what it is to be truly afraid but I may also experience moments of great joy. It will all be recorded.

Whatever happens, I will write.